Covet

Felicity Heaton

LONDON VAMPIRES SERIES

Covet
Crave
Seduce
Enslave
Bewitch
Unleash

Find out more at: www.felicityheaton.com

CHAPTER 1

There was one rule his kind honoured above all others: an owned human must never be touched by a vampire other than their master.

Every vampire knew that to lay a hand on a bonded human out of desire or feed from their vein caused them immeasurable pain and suffering, and that their master would know of it and would come to act out the penalty.

Death to the vampire who had broken the sacred law.

Death was not something that Javier was looking for but knowledge that it awaited him should he break the law hadn't stopped the fierce heat of desire from gripping him the moment she had arrived at the London theatre two years ago, sent to work by her master.

Javier had been telling himself to forget her ever since. In the time that she had been in the service of the theatre, he had been unable to escape the torment of her presence.

The simplest task had become agonizing for him.

Giving her orders for the night with the other staff was torture he couldn't endure.

Two years and his need for her had only grown worse. His desire had gone from a liquid fire that threatened to make him step out of line if he were in her presence for more than a minute to a crushing need to kiss her whenever he heard the soft melody of her voice in the distance.

It was unbearable.

But bear it he would.

There was no alternative. Her owner was one of the richest of Vampirerotique's patrons and his business partners would stake him if he lost the man's much needed money. That was, if the man didn't kill him first. Lord Ashville was an aristocrat, a pureblood vampire, and almost three times Javier's age and strength. As only an elite, Javier couldn't contend with him. His death would be swift and brutal, and by law he wasn't even allowed to defend himself. If he dared to touch her, to act out his dark urges and needs with the human female, he would have to quietly accept the consequences.

It was madness to desire a human owned by such a man. He would easily sense the violation of the bond. It was madness.

Javier swirled the blood in his crystal whisky glass, staring at it but not seeing it. His head was full of her, his heart rebelling against his better sense that said it was impossible and to give up on his futile desire for her. She would never be his.

The soft lighting in the back of the black limousine turned the blood dark and uninviting. He drank it anyway, forcing it down, and poured himself another glass from the decanter in the small refrigerator built into the back of the driver's seat. He had been drinking more and more often recently in the hope that it would stave off his growing hunger for her.

Lilah.

The car engine purred as they slowed and dread settled in his stomach.

This was the moment he always feared whenever he was called away from the theatre.

Lilah had been on his mind the whole time during his journey, and the whole month that he had been resident at his remote family home in northern Spain.

He could still see her clearly in his mind, could vividly remember how she had looked at him with her beautiful golden brown eyes when he had announced to the staff that he would be leaving them in the capable hands of Callum, and how her heart had set off at a pace, colouring her cheeks when his control had slipped and he had looked directly at her.

She was so beautiful, so alluring even in the plain long black dress of her uniform.

She had haunted him this past month, had been waiting for him to close his eyes each morning and drift off to sleep before stepping into his dreams and ensuring his desire for her burned fiercer than ever each night he awoke.

A month.

The car pulled to a halt on the road outside the elegant columned Grecian façade of the theatre. Warm floodlights lit the sandstone from below. On a normal night of business, it would have looked inviting to him, his home away from home, the place that housed something so precious to him. Tonight, it looked cold and dark, ominous and frightening.

An icy chill settled in his chest.

What if this time his fears became real and he had returned to find that she was gone?

A month was long enough for Lord Ashville to have decided he needed more servants in his mansion and sent for her. Callum had emailed Javier regular reports on the staff and the theatre while he had been away attending his sister's wedding.

His old friend hadn't mentioned Lilah at all but that didn't mean she was still here.

Javier had wanted to ask about her so many times, had typed the words in his emails to Callum only to delete them when sense had overcome the desires of his heart. Callum might understand his plight but if word reached Antoine or Snow, the aristocrat brothers who ran Vampirerotique with them, there would be hell to pay.

The car door opened and Javier swiftly necked the glass of blood. He set the glass down and stepped out of the limousine, his polished black leather shoes reflecting the lights of the theatre.

He straightened his deep silver-grey tie and fastened the button on his black suit jacket, preparing himself mentally at the same time. The driver nodded and closed the door, and then opened the boot of the vehicle and removed his luggage.

Javier took the dark grey suit bags from him, hanging them off his fingers by his side, and looked up at the theatre. Six tall columns supported a triangular block of sandstone.

Each carved figure on the frieze had been cleaned during his time away in preparation for the new season. Tonight was the first show, open only to elite vampires. The aristocrats were yet to return from the countryside or abroad.

Javier managed a smile when the wooden shutters on the other side of the windows and glass doors drew back, revealing the sumptuous red and gold interior of the theatre and his friend. Callum's steps were swift and sure, his handsome face a picture of darkness as he hurried down the wide marble staircase in the middle of the entrance hall, tying his long black hair back into a ponytail.

He shoved the doors open, leaving one of the staff to hurriedly wipe his handprints off the glass, and briskly took the five stone steps that led down to the pavement and Javier.

"It's a nightmare." Callum raked long fingers through his hair, messing it up again.

It was a habit of the elite vampire's when he was under stress. His green eyes flashed with irritation and Javier could sense that he was angry about something as well as see it.

"Hello to you too." Javier's smile widened and he motioned for the driver to come to him.

Callum snatched the black designer suitcase from the driver, stuffed a large tip in the man's breast pocket, and waved him away.

Like Javier, Callum wasn't used to the attention of servants and being waited on. It had taken them both years to get used to having humans and weaker vampires fetch them things or do menial tasks such as carrying their baggage.

Clearly Callum still had difficulty with the latter.

Javier looked beyond him to the foyer of the theatre, hoping to catch a glimpse of Lilah. Was she working tonight?

He frowned, his sandy eyebrows knitting tightly, and stared at Callum. What if his nightmare had something to do with the staff?

"Has something bad happened?" He fought to keep the note of worry from his voice. Callum would see straight through him if it slipped out.

They had spent years together at the finest vampire academy in England even though Callum was a century younger than he was and had remained in touch after graduating. They had always been close friends, even when they had been hundreds of miles apart and in two different countries.

"Victor got into a fight and got his nose broken. He's a bloody mess." Callum practically growled the words, his British accent hardening the final two and emphasising his anger.

Javier could understand his distress now.

Victor was one of their best performers and often took the lead in the final act of the show, seducing a human thrall before feeding from them in front of the audience.

He was a favourite among the female theatregoers because of his good looks and the fact that he was happy to engage with male as well as female partners on stage, and could handle more than one human at a time.

He had been with the theatre for almost a decade and was a big draw. Even the aristocrat females liked him and he wasn't averse to giving some of them private performances to keep them sweet and keep the money rolling in for the theatre.

They needed Victor on form and on stage.

On a normal night, Javier might have felt more concerned by the news, but the flight from Spain had felt as though it had taken days rather than a couple of hours and his frayed nerves were telling him to find somewhere quiet to rest, at least until he knew that Lilah was still here.

Still temptingly close.

Once he knew that, he would be able to function again and find his usual calm edge and the emotional balance he needed in order to face a crisis. He couldn't think straight at the moment, let alone deal with the drama of their star performer having a broken nose when he was due to go on stage tonight.

"So tell Antoine." Javier swept his suit bags over his shoulder, resting the back of his hand on the soft material of his black suit jacket. "He deals with the performers, not me."

"Antoine is busy with Snow, and I have good reason for coming to you first." Callum mounted the sandstone steps again and led the way into the brightly lit foyer of the theatre. The black haired elite vampire looked over his shoulder at Javier, his vivid green eyes still dark. "It was one of the staff who hit him."

"One of the staff broke his nose?" Javier found that one difficult to digest.

All of the staff were either human or of weak vampire lineage. Victor was of elite blood. His family weren't as strong as Javier's or Callum's, their blood diluted by too many turned humans in their ranks, but he was still powerful enough to deal with any of Javier's staff.

"A woman." Callum dumped Javier's expensive luggage down in the middle of the marble floor. He waved to one of the passing male staff and the man came over to them. "Take these things to Javier's office."

The man dutifully picked up the suitcase and then held his hand out to Javier. He stared at it.

"I was going to freshen up and change before the performance tonight. It has been a long journey, Callum. I'm sure this can wait."

The look on Callum's face said it wouldn't. Javier sighed and handed the dark grey suit bags to the man. He bowed his head, hurried across the foyer to the side of the double-height elegant room and opened the plain wooden door that led to the staff only areas of the theatre.

"The show starts in under an hour. We need to get Victor fixed up and then you need to speak with the woman who hit him and find out what happened before Antoine hears. He has enough problems on his plate at the moment. Snow is going through a rough patch again. I doubt he will tolerate this, regardless of who her owner is."

"Owner? The female is human?" Javier said and Callum nodded. "Who was it?"

Callum's dark eyebrows rose and he shrugged his broad shoulders, shifting his black designer suit jacket. "You know I'm not good with their names."

Javier knew that. Callum dealt with the darker side of the theatre business, tracking down vampires who could become good performers from cities all over Europe and sourcing human victims for the final act and other parts of the show the theatre hosted each week.

His friend had long ago given up finding out anything about the humans.

He had said it made his work easier.

Javier took that to mean that his old friend was growing a conscience about what he was doing. He had even given the sourcing of victims over to a firm of vampires recently, letting them deal with it all, and had focused on finding vampire performers to bring into the Vampirerotique family instead.

Callum started across the foyer in the direction the man had taken and Javier followed. An hour wasn't a long time to fix this mess without Antoine hearing about it.

If Snow was in a bad way again, Antoine would be in the mood for bloody murder. Whenever his older brother went off the rails, Antoine's temper degenerated into nothing short of vicious.

"Can you describe her?" Javier suspected that Callum would be able to manage that at least. He had an eye for detail, especially when it came to human females. The prettier the better to him.

"Tall, reddish brown hair... fiery... great tits... and had the strangest golden eyes."

Javier stopped dead.

Callum paused with his hand on the wooden door, holding it open, and looked back at him.

Lilah had hit Victor?

Before he could ask Callum more about it, a female member of staff appeared out of the gloom on the other side of the open door. She bowed her head to Callum, who still held the door, and then Javier and walked through.

Javier's gaze tracked her, his head tilting to one side as he took in what she was wearing.

"Do you like it?" Callum said and when Javier looked back at him, he was smiling, all trace of anger and concern gone from his eyes. "I thought it suited the theatre more and it means the staff can move around during the performances without being an eyesore for those attending."

Javier turned back to stare at the woman again. She stood near the glass doors, speaking to one of the male staff as he polished the windows.

"I leave you in charge for a month, and you change the uniforms?" Javier couldn't quite believe it. Callum thought that the incident with Victor was a nightmare. This was a nightmare to Javier.

The male uniform hadn't changed much. The material of the black formal outfit the man wore was a little finer than before, and the cut was tailored now so it fit snugly to his figure, but the long tail of the jacket still made him resemble a butler.

The female uniform.

Javier couldn't stop staring at it.

It looked as though Callum had gone to a sex shop and bought out every French maid uniform they had.

The puffed sleeves of the black dress were lined with black lace, and the neck scooped so low that Javier was surprised he couldn't see her nipples. Perhaps he could if he was close enough. The lace that trimmed the material there was probably obscuring them from this distance.

The horror of it didn't stop there.

The previous uniform dress had reached the ankle of the wearer. The new one barely reached mid-way down her thighs, revealing creamy flesh and long over-knee black socks. The only thing that had remained the same was the black pumps and the colour.

If he saw Lilah in such an outfit, it would be the death of him.

And he had to find her and find out why she had punched Victor.

The Devil help him, he wasn't going to be able to resist her any longer.

It would be a miracle if he even managed to utter a single question before finally succumbing to his need for her.

Callum's intent gaze on him roused him from his thoughts and he turned a blank look on him.

"You don't like it." Callum let the door drift shut. "We can change it back. I just thought it gave the guests something to look at between acts. Antoine thinks it's a good idea."

"I like it," Javier lied and forced another smile. "We should speak to Victor before Antoine comes down to speak to the performers prior to the show."

Javier hoped that Victor would tell them everything and then he wouldn't need to find Lilah and speak to her.

Callum opened the door again and Javier strode down the dimly lit black corridor with him, heading for the area to the side of the stage where stairs led up to the offices and hallways led backstage and off to the staff quarters.

They were almost at the end of the hallway and out into that brighter double-height expansive room when several females crossed before him. Lilah was among them, carrying a broom and a red plastic box of cleaning equipment, her dark chestnut hair twirled up in a bun at the back of her head.

She said something he didn't hear to the three other women and then broke away from them and struggled to open the heavy wooden doors that led to the area in front of the stage in the theatre.

Her broom knocked against the door when she managed to open it, fell from her grasp and clattered on the floor. She cursed softly and Javier echoed her in Spanish when she let the door close again and bent to retrieve her fallen broom.

The frilled black skirt of her dress hid nothing from view as she picked up the broom, her back to him. He stared at her bottom and her black knickers, blood pounding in his temples, his hunger for her kicking back into life and threatening to seize control of him.

He pictured crossing the scant few metres that separated them, sliding his hands over the firm peachy globes of her backside, and drawing her back against the raging erection tenting the black material of his tailored trousers beneath his jacket.

Lilah straightened so fast that he jumped and she whirled to face him.

Her cheeks coloured, rosy and dark, and the startled edge to her round eyes captivated him.

She blinked, shuttering her beautiful golden irises, and then dipped in a curtsey.

Her gaze stayed downcast this time, her head slightly to one side, so the cord of her neck remained taut and tempting.

"This is the one, Javier," Callum said and Javier almost barked that he knew that already and barely stopped himself from throttling his friend for interrupting his perusal of her neck.

He cleared his throat instead. "I will deal with you later."

Callum moved on. Javier remained where he was, his feet firmly planted to the dusty floor, his eyes glued to her, waiting to see her reaction.

Lilah's gaze slowly rose, bringing her head up with it. When it touched on his, the colour on her cheeks darkened and he forgot to breathe. He stared at her, mesmerised, lost in the black abyss of her dilated pupils.

Enthralled.

She didn't take her eyes away from his as expected. She held his gaze, steady and unafraid, no trace of fear in her scent. The way she looked at him spoke of desire and he had a hard time telling himself that he had to be imagining it. Her bond with her master made it impossible for her to feel anything for Javier.

The gentle rhythm of her heartbeat called to him, luring his gaze down to her cleavage, and he fought his desire to step closer so he could reach out and run a lone finger over the luscious curves of her breasts. Touching her would only bring her pain.

He couldn't.

No matter how much he needed to have her warm soft skin beneath his fingertips and know the feel of her at last. It would hurt her. He didn't care. No. He did care. If it hurt her, he would stop. He would never harm Lilah. To pain her was to pain himself. He cared about her too much.

"Are you coming?" Callum's voice shattered the spell she had cast on Javier and he glanced at him and nodded.

When he looked back, the door was closing and Lilah was gone.

He rubbed the bridge of his nose, drew in a long deep breath, catching the enticing scent of her in the air, and followed Callum backstage.

Later.

He would be in her presence. Alone.

And he wouldn't be able to resist her any longer.

If it hurt her, he would stop, but he needed to touch her.

He needed to know the feel of her and her taste.

Even if that one taste was all he could ever have.

Even if it signed his death sentence.

CHAPTER 2

Lilah didn't pause to watch the show as she cleaned the boxes, preparing the red velvet seats for the coming week. She pulled another of the covers off the plush soft seats and hit it with the palm of her hand to beat out any dust that had managed to creep under the protective cream material.

The murmur of the crowd below drew her attention to them. She pressed her hands into the small of her back, stretching her spine, and sighed.

Preparations for the new season were always tiring but she had been working harder than ever tonight, hoping that Callum would notice and that Javier's punishment would be less severe because of it.

She wasn't sorry that she had hit Victor. She was surprised.

She had expected him to stop her or evade her fist. He must have been more caught up in what he had been doing than she had thought.

Lilah removed the cover off the final chair in the elegant gold and red box, folded it and set it down on the pile near the red velvet curtain that shielded the private area from the corridor that ran between all the boxes. During the main season, the aristocrat vampires used the boxes, separating themselves from the elite who sat in the rows of seats filling the theatre below. She had never cleaned the boxes before.

She ran her fingers over the carved wooden top of the hip-height wall around the box. Antoine had arranged the cleaning of the exterior and repainting of the interior during the closed period so the cream paint was perfect, highlighted with beautiful gold that one of the decorators had told her was real. Only the best for the aristocrats.

Lilah leaned against the edge of the box and looked down at the crowd as they watched the show on the grand stage to her left.

How did the aristocrats feel when they sat up here, looking down on their weaker kin?

Was that why they preferred the boxes? So they could look down on vampires they believed were weaker and less worthy than they were?

She had never understood the sense of separation between them. To her, it didn't matter how pure their blood was or what lineage they were from. They were all vampires.

She had never believed in their existence until Lord Ashville had found her on the streets and forced his blood down her throat, bonding with her and claiming her as a sort of slave.

His blood in her veins linked her to him but she hadn't seen him in a long time and she didn't care. She hated him and wished she could break free of his rule, had tried to escape his mansion many times, so many that he had grown tired of her and sent her here along with another of his humans.

She hadn't realised what sort of place the theatre was until she had caught her first glimpse of the show. She had blushed a thousand shades of red and hadn't been able to take her eyes off the stage, watching the perversion playing out on it, the bloodletting and debauched erotic acts.

Lilah was used to it now and rarely stopped to watch, and she made sure that she was never in sight of the stage during the final act. The first time she had witnessed that, she had discovered the true nature of vampires.

The scent of human blood had driven them into a frenzy, both the vampires on stage and those in the audience. It had even reduced the aristocrats, with their fine airs and graces, to slavering beasts, their red eyes bright and sharpened fangs dripping with saliva.

That was the reason why she didn't understand the separation between elite and aristocrat. When it came down to it, all of them hungered for human blood and couldn't resist the smell of it. They were all beasts in human form.

A brief flicker of golden light drew her gaze down to the door below the boxes opposite her, close to the front of the stage. The door slowly shut and she shifted her focus forwards, past Antoine where he stood to one side watching the show, blending into the darkness that edged the theatre, to the vampire who had exited from backstage.

Javier.

It was dark where he crossed the theatre using the strip of open red carpet between the raised black stage and the front row of the audience, but she knew it was him.

She would recognise his fine athletic figure anywhere and the haphazard mess of his sandy brown hair. His suit jacket was gone but other than that he hadn't changed from when she had seen him earlier. Her heart had lodged in her throat when she had looked up to find him there, watching her, his rich chocolate eyes intent on her and stirring heat in her veins.

She had thought he would say something about what she had done, would berate her in front of everyone, and had even braced herself for the hard edge his words would have.

When he had spoken, his tone had been surprisingly soft, warm with his Spanish accent lacing the words. She could listen to him forever, sometimes drifted away when he was issuing orders to the staff first thing in the evening and last thing in the morning, imagining him speaking close to her ear.

Just the memory of his voice had her heartbeat accelerating, a flush of heat sweeping over her skin. Her teeth teased her lower lip. She had to stop torturing herself like this.

Javier would never do such a thing with her. He had taken care of her over the past two years but he took care of all his staff, whether they were vampire or human. She wasn't special to him.

Lilah leaned forwards, following him until he disappeared beneath her. Was he coming up?

He had said that he would speak to her later about what she had done. She both feared it and looked forward to it.

She picked up the broom again, intending to sweep the floor so she would look busy if Javier was coming to see her, but her gaze caught on the show.

Three men were pleasuring one woman in the middle of the luxurious red and gold stage set, all of them vampires right now, but she knew that would change before the final act. It was early in the show. With each act, things grew a little more risqué and a lot darker.

The moans of the four vampires writhing naked on stage filled the theatre, the rapt audience watching in silence.

The woman sat reclined on a red velvet armchair, her legs splayed over the arms and a man between them. Another stood to one side of her, one hand tangled in her blonde hair, holding her mouth to his cock as he thrust into it, his other hand on the erection of the man behind the armchair, pumping it as he kissed him.

Lilah tried to drag her eyes away but found that she couldn't when another two women joined the group, both of them human and both of them under the thrall of two of the vampires on stage.

She could tell it by their glassy expressions.

They walked calmly forwards on black stiletto heels, their sheer feather-trimmed baby dolls barely concealing their breasts and the black leather thongs they wore.

Two of the naked men broke away from the vampire female as the third man pulled her onto her knees on the armchair and thrust into her from behind, causing her to cry out.

The two female humans approached the male vampires who held them under their thrall, teetering on the heels now, a hint of nerves flickering on their faces. The males were lessening their control over them, letting them see where they were and that an audience was watching them.

The scent of their fear would satisfy the gathered elite and the humans would still be under the vampires' spells enough that they wouldn't think to escape.

The human women sat down on the two red leather couches positioned in the middle of the stage, one on each. Crimson spotlights bathed them, making them look as though blood covered their skin.

In perfect synchronisation, the broad bare male vampires crouched before their woman, lifted the opposite leg to each other and started to kiss along it from ankle to knee.

It wasn't turning her on.

Lilah told herself it a thousand times over but the sight of the vampire couple fornicating at the front of the stage and the forced seduction happening behind them had her heart pounding and her nipples hardening against the tight top of her uniform dress.

"I need to question you about Victor." Javier's deep accented voice coming from behind her caused her to drop her broom and turn.

She panted hard, startled and trying to get her arousal under control so he wouldn't sense it.

His dark brown gaze slid to the stage and then back to her.

Lilah quickly bent to pick up her broom. When she straightened, Javier's eyes were on her dress, his pupils wide in the low light coming up from below. The moans on stage grew louder and she tried to ignore them and push the images of the couples out of her mind.

"Why did you hit Victor?" Javier said, more composed than she was. Didn't the show affect him at all? He had crossed the theatre without pausing to watch and his eyes were fixed on her now. She had heard that he and his partners had been running the theatre for almost a century. He had probably grown immune to whatever was playing out on the stage.

"Because he was hurting Nia." It came out blunter than she had intended and she added, "Sir."

Javier's eyebrow rose. "Victor said you had no grounds to strike him."

"Then he's a liar and a bastard."

"He's an elite." The darkness in his tone was reprimand enough to Lilah. She bowed her head.

"My apologies." She couldn't bring herself to look at Javier so she glanced to one side when she brought her head back up. It was a mistake. The act on stage was getting hotter, with the two humans now kneeling on the couches and swallowing the rigid cocks of their partners as they stood before them. She ripped her gaze away and closed her eyes, figuring it was safer. That way she didn't risk seeing the anger in Javier's eyes or the debauchery on stage, and she could keep a clear head. "He was forcing himself on Nia and she told him to stop. When he didn't, I hit him. I thought he might stop and block me."

"He said Nia was cut. He was under the influence of his hunger. That is why he didn't stop."

That made sense. "Nia cut her hand on some glass. A mirror in the main dressing room had broken. We had to clean it up and she cut herself."

He muttered a ripe curse in Spanish and stepped towards her. "Were you cut?"

Lilah opened her eyes, looked up into the dark pools of his, and shook her head. "No."

The relief that swamped his eyes surprised her and sent fear into her blood. What if she had been the one to cut herself? Would Victor have tried to touch her and taste her instead? Would Nia have tried to stop him or would she have let him hurt her?

"You must be more careful around our kind," Javier said and she nodded slowly, unable to take her eyes off his.

The moans from the stage grew louder and she blushed when Javier looked towards the performance.

"Will I be punished?" She tried to shut out the sounds. Javier's gaze returned to her and he shook his head.

"Victor overstepped the line." He frowned and turned quiet for so long that she couldn't ignore the noises coming from the stage. She glanced across at them. Javier's voice dropped to a whisper. "Do you like to watch them?"

Her eyes shot wide and she instantly shook her head. He stepped closer, slid his hand over her jaw in a way that had her shivering and her breath quaking, and carefully turned her face towards the stage. His thumb and fingers remained against her face, holding her gently, warming her down to her bones and causing a flood of arousal to sweep through her.

He traced his hand down her throat and stepped up behind her.

What was he doing?

She trembled under his touch, anticipating pain from it but feeling nothing but pleasure.

"Does it arouse you when you watch them fucking?" he breathed into her ear and she shivered, her eyelids dropping, a ripple of shock running over her skin at hearing him say such a thing.

"I don't watch them," she whispered, her voice barely there.

"You were watching them when I arrived." He ran his thumb up her throat and claimed her jaw again.

How long had he been watching her before he had said something and torn her attention away from the show?

Had he enjoyed watching her while she watched the performance, unaware of his presence and his eyes on her?

The thought that he might have sent heat into her blood that pooled in her abdomen, tightening it with arousal.

She couldn't take her eyes off the show now but she wasn't taking any of it in. All of her focus was on Javier where he stood behind her, so close that his hip was against her bottom.

Why was he doing this? Why wasn't it hurting her? Was there no pleasure in his touch, no sense of desire inside him as he ran his hands over her throat and pressed his body close to hers?

Lilah sharply turned her head towards him. He was so close to her that his breath skated over her lips, her chin touching his cheek. The darkness of desire in his eyes was unmistakable. There was hunger in his touch, in the way he forced her to face the stage again, clutching her jaw and lowering his mouth to her throat.

He drew in a long shaky breath and pressed his brow against the side of her head. "You smell so good... such a temptation."

He wanted her. Her knees weakened beneath her, legs going slack at the feel of him pressed against her back, his hands firm on her body.

Lilah's breathing quickened and she stared at the three couples on stage, her heart racing and blood thundering.

Javier reached around her and slid his hand over hers where it gripped the pole of the broom. He took it from her and let it fall to the ground as he pressed soft kisses to her bare shoulder and the nape of her neck. They tickled, sending shiver after shiver through her, dizzying her.

This was so wrong.

But that only made it feel more right.

She had wanted him for so long, had craved the feel of his hands on her body, ached to know what it would feel like to be with him. She had never thought it possible though, had thought her bond to Lord Ashville would prevent it and pain her if she accepted the touch of the man she desired with all of her heart.

Javier licked the nape of her neck near her hairline, teasing her, and she couldn't stop herself from arching her backside into him. He groaned and cursed softly in her ear, kissing it and nibbling it with blunt teeth.

"Watch them," he whispered into her ear and licked the lobe, teasing it with the tip of his tongue. "Keep watching them while I touch you."

She nodded and bit back a groan when he slid his hands down over her stomach and then around to her backside, palming it through her short dress. He suckled the lobe of her ear and then kissed her throat and ran his hands up her sides, pressing them in hard as he passed over her ribs. He cupped her breasts and stepped into her.

The feel of his erection against her bottom sent a new hot flood of arousal pooling between her thighs.

Was this really happening?

She felt as though she was imagining it, as though it was a fevered fantasy brought on by watching the show and seeing him crossing the theatre towards her. It didn't feel real.

"You cannot deny me this," he uttered into her ear and she trembled at the command in his tone, the hunger that roughened it. "I will have you."

Lilah didn't want to deny him, but the thought that he wouldn't let her only served to arouse her further, making her heart skip a beat as his strong hands kneaded her breasts through the confines of her short black dress.

She would never deny him.

No matter the consequences.

He was worth the risk.

And she would have him.

CHAPTER 3

Lilah almost covered her mouth to contain her moan as Javier squeezed her breasts, thumbing her nipples through the black material of her dress. She leaned back into him, trying to keep her eyes on the show, struggling to focus on it as he had told her to when he was setting her aflame with his touch. He groaned against her throat and licked the nape of her neck again, tickling and teasing her.

Her eyelids dropped when he skimmed his hands downwards, pressing them in hard when he reached her stomach and flattening his palms against her. He continued this time, his mouth dropping to the back of her shoulder as his hands reached the end of the skirt of her dress.

He moaned again, apparently uncaring that there was an audience below them, watching the same show that she was. It was exciting to do this with him in the privacy of the box, courting the risk of someone seeing them, watching them as everyone else watched the performance.

He muttered something about the feel of her thighs and the sight of her in the dress and swept his hands along the length of her bare arms. She frowned when he lifted her hands and placed them on the curved edge of the box and held them there. He pressed his body against the full length of hers, resting his chin on her shoulder.

"Still watching?" he whispered and she nodded, her eyes fixed on the three couples below.

They were writhing together now, swapping partners, an erotic vision of lust as they licked, palmed, suckled and touched each other on the decadent gold and red set.

Her breathing quickened again, chest heaving against the tight dress, her body alive with hunger and need, with the ache to feel Javier's hands on her flesh, re-enacting what was happening below them on the stage.

Javier skimmed his strong hands down to her hips and raised her short skirt, his fingers curling the material into his fists. He tugged it up to her waist and slipped his hands downwards again, caressing her thighs.

She gasped as he cupped her mound, holding it and drawing her backwards. He ground himself against her backside, the material of his trousers like silk against her bottom. He was so hard and she was so wet for him, throbbing with the need to feel him inside her, filling her just as the men on stage were filling the women with their long rigid cocks.

His hand shifted against her, rubbing her through her panties, worsening her ache for him. His other hand caressed upwards, trailing over her thigh and skimming along the waist of her underwear. He kissed her shoulder and whispered dark things against her skin, things that only made her want him even more.

"Do you want me inside you like that?" he breathed into her ear and she stared at the men on stage, watching as they took the women from behind, some of them bent over the red leather couches. She swallowed but could only manage a short moan as her response. "I want to be inside you. I've wanted it forever."

God. She wanted it too.

She quivered under his erotic touch, writhing against his hand, seeking some relief from the pressure building inside her. She imagined what it would feel like when he finally claimed her body, plunging his cock in hard, his strong arms caging her against his body.

It would be more arousing than anything she was seeing on the stage. She only hoped that this private performance didn't end as the one below was due to—with bloodshed and death.

"Keep watching," Javier whispered and then kissed her ear and slipped his hand into the front of her panties.

Lilah gasped and moaned, her breath hitching in her throat at the first touch of his fingers. He slid his hand into her plush wet petals, teasing her clit, and she leaned backwards into him, melting in his arms. He held her and ground against her backside again, thrusting harder this time.

"So wet," he groaned and bit her neck with blunt teeth, staying there a moment as though he couldn't bear to move.

He swirled his finger around her, then growled and suddenly pulled his hand out.

Lilah jumped and clutched the edge of the box as he yanked her panties down to her ankles. He was rough as he pulled them off, tugging each of her feet up so swiftly that she almost fell. Her heart thundered, blood rushing through her head, colliding with her need for him and making her dizzy.

He pushed the skirt of her dress up and groaned again as he kneaded her backside.

He came to stand behind her and she shivered when she heard him unzip his trousers.

This was really happening.

She swallowed to wet her dry mouth and shift the lump from her throat. Her hands trembled, thighs quivering when he touched them, his hands firm against her flesh.

He lifted her right leg and placed her foot on the curved wall of the box, exposing her to the draught of the theatre.

The moans from the stage grew more heated but she still held her own inside, fighting the urge to join them.

Javier didn't hold back.

He groaned as he caressed her thighs and his moan deepened when he reached her pussy. His touch was too much for her, bringing her too close to the edge. As if sensing that, he moved his hands away from her crotch and around to her bottom again.

When he touched her this time, it was with the head of his cock. He ran it down the crack of her backside, his breath cool and fast against her back and the nape of her neck, coming out in short pants.

She tried to keep her eyes open but anticipation made it impossible.

They slipped shut with the first caress of his hard length over her pussy and she bit her lip and tilted her head back as he ran the blunt head along her wet cleft, teasing and torturing her with it. It brushed the opening of her slick channel and then moved away, running up her backside again, sweeping over her anus.

She couldn't contain the moan then.

It slipped free, low and hungry, and Javier groaned in response.

He nudged against her bottom, enough to tease her into wondering what it might be like to experience such a thing, and then lowered himself again.

"You're not watching the show," he said and she forced her eyes open, fixing them on the act.

Her teeth pressed into her lower lip.

One of the males had taken centre stage, his female bent over before him. She clutched her knees, her backside high in the air, her blonde hair a curtain over her face.

Lilah swallowed as the man took hold of his rigid length and nudged the head of it into the woman.

The blunt crown of Javier's cock entering her almost had her closing her eyes again but she kept them open, felt him easing into her inch by delicious inch as the man entered the woman below.

Her moan joined the woman's as Javier thrust the last few inches of his thick cock hard into her core, burying himself deep, stretching her body to accommodate him.

Lilah sighed and focused on the feel of him inside her, claiming her body.

It felt so right.

She gripped the edge of the box and leaned forwards, arching her back so Javier could go deeper, could claim all of her.

He groaned and ran one hand down her back, forcing her further forwards. Her hip hurt but she didn't care. She kept her right foot on the wall and her eyes on the show as he pulled out of her and eased back in, stretching her and reaching deep inside.

He moaned again, uttering her name in a low sexy voice that made her tremble with a need to answer him.

"Javier," she whispered and her lips parted, breath leaving her on a low groan as he thrust into her again.

He ran his hands over her bottom and lifted her skirt, exposing her backside to the cool air. She tiptoed as he began to thrust, his fingers curling around her hips, clutching her and holding her in place. He wasn't gentle but wasn't as rough as she had expected. He plunged deep and hard into her, burying the full length of his cock and causing his balls to smack against her pussy.

It was thrilling and every bit as exciting as she had anticipated as she watched the show, watched the man on stage fucking the woman while Javier took her, filling her with rough desperate strokes of his long cock.

His grip on her hips tightened, his groans so low she could barely hear them.

She couldn't contain hers any longer.

They fell from her lips, interspersed with his name as he plunged into her, his pace quickening as she started to clench him, seeking her pleasure.

Fear that someone would hear them only added to the thrill of it all.

Javier muttered things she didn't understand, his voice harsh and guttural, divinely commanding. He pressed his left hand into her stomach, pulled her up against him, and kept pumping her, thrusting his length as deep as he could go as if he wanted to possess her, to ruin her to all others.

She moaned and leaned back into him, letting him at her throat. He whispered profanities against it and licked and sucked, devouring it with his lips as he took her, his thrusts turning rougher and more desperate. He placed his mouth on the curve of her neck and she could feel his desire to bite her, could sense the need ripple through him.

He stayed there as he plunged into her and she yearned to feel the press of his fangs against her flesh, could barely breathe with the anticipation.

He cursed softly and kissed back down to her shoulder. His free hand covered her pussy again, fingers seeking her clit, and he circled it as he filled her roughly with his cock, thrusting hard and fast.

Lilah couldn't hold on any longer.

It was too much as she tensed around his length and he pumped into her. She moaned loud enough she was sure that someone would have heard her and fell apart, quivering all over and barely able to remain standing as her orgasm crashed through her, heat chasing outwards from her core and carrying her away.

Javier stilled inside her, his groans low and barely audible over the noise of the performance. He remained there for a few seconds, as though absorbing the feel of her body trembling because of him, and then withdrew.

Lilah frowned.

She didn't understand.

Javier carefully lowered her leg for her, turned her around and leaned her against the curved wall of the box. He eased to a crouch before her, picked up her discarded black panties, and slipped them back over her feet. She watched him, heart hammering and head still reeling, trying to grasp what was happening. She shivered when he finished dressing her and caressed the front of her knickers.

He hadn't climaxed.

His hard cock jutted out of his open trousers, wet with her juices and dark with need.

"Someone would know," he said, as though it was a reasonable explanation for leaving himself unsatisfied.

It was completely unreasonable to her. She didn't care if anyone smelt him on her and she was sure that the one person who she didn't want to know was already aware of what she had done with Javier. Lord Ashville.

Javier stood and went to tuck his erection into his trousers. She stopped him by touching his hand and he looked at her. The longer lengths of his sandy hair on top of his head had fallen forwards, masking one dark eye. She took his hand away from his cock and moved to kneel in front of him. He groaned and shook his head but it didn't stop her.

Lilah licked his thick length, tasting herself, and took him into her mouth. He groaned and tensed, his hips bucking forwards. She closed her eyes and sucked him, rolling her tongue around the blunt head each time she withdrew, hoping to drive him out of his mind.

He was cool under her tongue, rock hard with desire, and she rubbed her thighs together, her sated body starting to ache with need again. Each moan he loosed only added to her arousal. She sucked harder and he grabbed her shoulders, uttering her name in the most delicious way, driving her on.

She quickened her pace, swiftly swallowing his cock and then sucking hard each time she withdrew. His hands trembled on her shoulders, alternating between clutching her and pushing against her, as though he wanted her to stop. She wouldn't. Not until he felt as satisfied as she did.

He groaned her name again and she looked up at him. He was watching her rather than the show and the feel of his eyes on her only heightened her growing arousal. She wanted to feel him inside her again, pumping his seed into her as he came, claiming her body as his.

Javier growled and shot his load into her mouth, his cock throbbing and hips thrusting shallowly. His eyes changed, pupils narrowing and stretching, turning elliptical, and red flooding his irises. The sight of them and his fangs as he breathed hard and fast, coming down from his climax, frightened her a little but she refused to look away. She sat back on her heels and stared up into his eyes, seeing him for what he was.

Not a vampire.

Just the man she had been slowly falling for these past two years.

His pupils gradually changed back, the crimson drained from his irises, and his fangs receded. He continued to stare at her, his breathing heavy and trousers down around his knees.

Javier swallowed, held his hand out to her, and pulled her up onto her feet.

For a moment, she thought that he would kiss her.

He smoothed her clothes down, tucked himself away and fastened his trousers. He lifted his hand as though he was going to touch her face, curled his fingers into a fist and lowered it again. A soft curse left his lips and he turned and walked away.

Lilah stared at the red velvet curtain of the box as it fell back into place. She leaned against the low curved wall and listened to the crowd applaud as the show ended, feeling bereft and confused.

Was that all he was going to give her?

It wasn't enough.

She needed more than just one brief moment with him and had done since the first night she had seen him. He had to feel that way too. She had caught him watching her more than once and had always wondered what he was thinking to make his eyes so dark and full of hunger.

Now she knew and she wanted more of him.

She wanted to see that look in his brown eyes again and know that he wanted her and needed her with the same ferocity as she needed him.

She couldn't just let him walk away.

Wouldn't.

She knew the consequences of what they had done and she feared for him and for herself, but it was too late to turn back now. They had crossed the line and she was going to make the most of every second she had with Javier. She would savour them all and would face her master with him when the time came.

Lilah grabbed her broom and her cleaning equipment, tucked the seat covers under her arm, and hurried from the box. She raced along the red-walled hallway heading for the stairs down to the next floor, and then the next.

When she reached the bottom, she dumped the covers in the waiting trolley and dropped her red plastic box and broom. She shoved the mahogany doors that led to backstage and rushed through them.

It was pandemonium backstage. The vampires from tonight's performance were discussing the show and the two males who had been with the human females paused to watch her as she passed. One of them wiped the back of his hand across his bloodied mouth and sniffed. Lilah kept her head down and kept moving, aware that they could smell Javier on her.

Her cheeks blazed.

She wished they could smell him inside her as she had wanted him to be. She broke into a run, passing the stacks of props, and reached the other side of the stage. She didn't stop running until she had reached Javier's office on the ground floor. Her hand shook as she knocked. No answer.

She hesitated before opening the door. He wasn't there.

Lilah closed the door and headed through the black-walled double-height room to the stairs. She had cleaned the apartments of the owners once before and knew where his was.

She moved as quickly as her legs could carry her but they were tiring now, weak from supporting her in an unusual position while Javier had driven her to the most mind-blowing orgasm she'd ever had.

She slowed to a walk as she reached the top floor of the building and the beautifully decorated black and gold hallway that ran between the four large apartments. Lilah hesitated when a snarl sounded from one of the rooms close to her. It wasn't Javier. His apartment was at the end of the corridor.

She held her breath and snuck towards the door, afraid that it would open. She knew who lived in that apartment. When she had come to clean them that one time, the vampire who occupied it had turned her away, telling her that it wasn't safe for her to be around him.

She had never seen anything like him.

His overlong white hair and startling red eyes had shocked her.

Snow.

She had heard all sorts of rumours about him since then. He was old and dangerous, prone to dark moods in which he could drain three humans dry and still hunger for more. His brother was the only one allowed in his room. He was liable to kill anyone else who tried to enter.

Lilah pressed against the wall opposite and didn't look back when she was past his door. She hurried to the end of the hall and knocked on the mahogany panelled door there.

No one answered.

Lilah knocked again.

The door finally opened and Javier stood before her.

Her nerve failed and her gaze drifted from his eyes, down the slope of his straight nose to his bowed mouth. It lingered there for a second before she dragged it away, across to his left ear. It caught on the start of a thin silver scar just below his earlobe and she followed that down over the cords of his neck to the middle of his left pectoral. From there, her eyes roamed over the enticing display of hard honed muscle barely hidden beneath milk-white skin. It drifted over the ridges of his abdomen, past the dip of his navel, to the dark thatch of hair that led her gaze downwards.

To the top of a black towel tied around his waist.

Was he going to shower?

Had he intended to scrub her scent off his body as though that could erase what they had done?

That hurt her and she didn't know what to say as he stared at her.

If she told him what she wanted, if she confessed her deepest desires and what she kept hidden in her heart, would he turn her away or would he say the words she needed to hear?

Would he tell her that it was just the show and the heat of the moment?

Or would he confess that he felt something for her too?

CHAPTER 4

Javier remained still as Lilah stared down at the black towel slung low around his hips, telling his body not to start getting the wrong idea. It wasn't a good time for it to slip free of his control. He needed to keep a firm grip on it even though the sight of Lilah in the tight short black dress and the scent of him on her was driving him closer to the edge with each passing second.

"Were you going to shower?" The tremble in her voice along with the agitation in her blood gave away her muddled feelings and when she finally raised her golden eyes to meet his, he could see the edge of hurt in them and knew what she was really asking.

Was he going to wash away her scent?

He didn't want to wash the smell of her off his skin. He wanted to keep it on him until the passing of time rendered it beyond his senses, wanted to lose himself in her so that moment never happened and so he would forever smell of Lilah's sweet fragrance.

He needed it with a ferocity that astounded him. He longed for her to belong to him even when it was impossible. Her master would have known the moment he had given up his fight for control and touched her tonight. He had violated the sacred law and sentenced himself, and nothing he did now could save him.

Nothing he did now could make things worse either.

Javier stepped aside, holding the door for her. "Come in before someone sees you and wonders what you're doing here. I'm in enough trouble as it is."

Lilah remained standing on the threshold of his room. He sighed, reached out, took her hand and pulled her into the room. He felt her tense when he slammed the door and she remained with her back to him, her wrist held tight in his grip, so fragile beneath his fingers.

So delicate.

She was a rare flower and he felt as though she had bloomed for him tonight, had filled his dark world with the scent of her intoxicating fragrance and given it colour for a brief moment.

He wanted that again.

Needed it.

Needed her.

"Where is your master?" he whispered and turned towards her, his gaze on his hand where it held her wrist.

The sight of his fingers locked around her, touching her at last, fascinated him. He had wanted this for so long that he couldn't deny his desire for her. Even this simple touch was too much for him, filled him with hunger and flooded his veins with the heat of passion.

He wanted to pull her against him, twist her into his arms, and kiss her. His gaze dropped to her rosy lips and he realised that he hadn't touched them yet.

They were virgin territory, too pure to taint with his. He feared he would ruin them, would lose control of himself and his need and would cut them so he could taste her delicate blood in the kiss. He wasn't worthy of touching them. He was a beast and no matter how much he desired this beauty, she was beyond his grasp.

She belonged to another.

But neither of them were worthy of her.

Javier fought the desire to fall to his knees before her and beg for her forgiveness, to confess now before her master came to claim his head that he had loved her from afar for these two years, that she had captivated and ruined him to all others from the moment she had walked into his life.

So innocent.

So pure.

So beautiful.

He needed her to know that he wasn't a beast, that whatever she thought of his kind, he was different to them and would do all in his power to protect her from the cruelty and darkness in his world. He would free her from it if he could.

What good could he do for her now though? He had sealed his fate tonight.

It was over.

He had killed himself and hurt her in the process. He was a beast.

Javier's legs gave out and his knees hit the wooden floor, the force of impact jolting his spine. Lilah gasped and was before him in an instant, crouching close with her hand on his shoulder.

"Are you sick?"

A mirthless chuckle escaped him. Perhaps he was. He had been so cruel to her, and he had said that he loved her. A man in love would have thought about her and placed her first, would have protected her even from himself and spared her the pain of his touch.

Her soft hand shifted to his face, settling against his cheek, and he closed his eyes and leaned into the caress.

It was too much to hope that her master was so far away that he wouldn't have sensed what Javier had done tonight.

It was too much to hope that he had more than a few hours left on Earth.

If she would let him, he would spend his last hours with her.

It would hurt her.

Javier lifted his eyes to hers and the concern in them healed some of the pain in his heart. Could she feel something for him too? It wasn't possible. Her bond to her master saw to that.

"I am sorry if I hurt you earlier," he whispered, voice fractured and hoarse.

He ached to raise his hand and cover hers, to hold it to his face and press a kiss to her palm, to tip his chin up and claim the lips that tempted him so much and ruin her.

A smile curved those lips, pure and full of the feelings in her eyes. They were soft with understanding.

"You were a little rough at times but I enjoyed it," she said in an equally soft and alluring voice, capturing him in the spell of it for a moment before her words sank in and confused him.

"No... I mean if my desire for you caused you pain."

Lilah fell quiet, the light leaving her beautiful eyes until they reflected his confusion. Her voice was a bare whisper when she finally spoke. "It should have then? It didn't."

Javier slumped further, his hands on his knees, his mind racing. "Why?"

Lilah shook her head. "I don't know. I thought maybe someone had been lying to me about it... that it was something we were told to keep us in line and obedient."

"It's the truth, Lilah," he said and her cheeks coloured. Did she like the way he said her name? She blushed whenever he dared to use it. "I should have hurt you."

"Maybe it was because I wanted you too."

That surprised him more than the fact that she hadn't experienced pain from his touch.

"That's another thing. You shouldn't want me... the bond should prevent it."

Her eyes widened. "Oh."

They sat in silence for too long. Javier tried to think of something to say to chase away the clouds that were gathering in her eyes. He could feel her anger rising as she stared down at his towel. What could he say to make that hurt go away? He didn't know what was upsetting her. Perhaps discovering that would be a good starting point.

"What are you thinking?"

Her gaze crept back up to his and then she turned her face away and stared at the floor off to his right, exposing the smooth column of her throat to his hungry eyes.

"Javier... was it just the heat of the moment... or do you... do you feel something for me too?"

Javier couldn't breathe.

She stole it away with the confirmation that he wasn't the only one who harboured feelings beyond lust and desire for the person opposite him.

He stared at her, hungry to touch her again and prove to her that what had happened hadn't been because of the show. It was because he loved her. He had fought it so hard, had done all he could to hold back his need for her and his desire, but in the end his struggle had been in vain. There was no going back now.

She closed her eyes when he touched her cheek and he sighed when she leaned into the caress, her skin warming his palm.

"I have wanted you forever," he whispered and her eyes slowly opened and shyly met his. He frowned. "Lilah... do you know where your master is?"

The warmth in her eyes flickered and died, replaced by a cold abyss and darkness that surprised him. He hoped that her master was outside the range at which he could sense her. It was a slim chance but it was all that he had.

"The bastard isn't in London, that's for sure," she snapped and glared at him, her expression as black as midnight.

Javier felt as though he was looking at a different person. Gone was his beautiful rose, replaced by a thorny thistle. Her loathing and anger flowed into him through his hand on her face. It obliterated the sweetness of her blood and turned the scent of it bitter.

"My skin crawls whenever he's nearby."

Javier frowned at her, shocked by her tone. Most owned humans were deferential to their masters, obedient and grateful for the beneficial effects of their blood. Lord Ashville's blood in her body granted Lilah protection against most diseases and slowed her aging.

He stroked her cheek and some of the darkness in her eyes lifted. "Do you hate your master, Lilah?"

"I never asked to be his. He gave me no choice in the matter. Isn't he supposed to give me a choice?" Lilah looked away, shame burning her cheeks, heating his palm.

Tears lined her dark lashes, threatening to slip and fall onto his hand.

His heart ached for her and her suffering.

Lord Ashville had bonded with her against her will. It was unheard of in vampire society. A human had to enter willingly into the contract with their vampire master.

Javier slid his hand around the back of her neck and drew her to him. She fell against his bare chest, her head in the curve of his neck with her forehead brushing his throat and her hands pressing into his pectorals.

Bliss.

He had never experienced such euphoria. He wrapped his arms around her and closed his eyes, savouring the feel of her in his embrace and the warmth of her against him.

Would she have ever asked to be anyone's?

Would she have ever consented to be his?

"Javier... is it different if I'm acting against my master... if I choose to sleep with you?" she whispered and it felt as though she had heard the questions in his heart, as if it had spoken them to hers and she had voiced her answer to them.

He held her closer to him, breathing her in, making the most of this stolen moment with her.

He had lived six centuries in this world and had never found anyone like Lilah. She was a little piece of Heaven in his arms, brought colour to his world and turned it into a paradise. Even if their time together was only this night, it had been worth waiting six hundred years for.

Lilah drew back, her hands still against his chest, burning his skin with their soft touch, and looked up into his eyes. "If he doesn't have enough power over me to stop me from doing as I please... are we still breaking the law?"

"I don't know." Javier was certain that no one else at the theatre would know the answer to that question either. Snow was the oldest, over two thousand years old, but Javier doubted even he could tell them whether they were free of the law. It was too much to hope for and Lord Ashville wouldn't care about such technicalities when he came to act out his vengeance. "Most owned humans don't struggle against the thrall of their bond to their master. It is a violation of their will if another vampire touches them, something that pains them greatly. You are different. Lord Ashville might have given you blood, but no sacred bond lies between you. I am not sure what that means... but if he felt what happened tonight, he will still be coming for me."

Lilah lowered her gaze again and then looked back into his eyes. "Perhaps if we made sure that I was the one breaking the law and not you... if the rules speak only of a vampire violating them, not the human, then if I'm the one to initiate things... wouldn't we be safe?"

The idea that she was planning to sleep with him again wrought havoc on his body, causing an intense wave of desire to roll through him, destroying all sense of control in its wake. His heart said to kiss this angel who offered herself so freely to him but his mind overruled it and forced a reminder from his lips.

"I already violated them."

She frowned. "We can say that was me too... I won't let him touch you... I won't let him take you from me, Javier."

Javier stared at her, lost in her eyes and the force behind her words. The sound of his name on her lips echoed around his head and warmed his heart.

A touch of rose slowly coloured her cheeks and she went to look away from him.

He caught her cheek, holding her steady so her gaze remained on his, and swallowed. He wasn't sure whether her claiming to have initiated things between them would make a difference. He wanted to tell her that but she leaned towards him and as flimsy as her logic was, he couldn't resist her.

She dropped her hands to his knees, pushed herself up, and brought her mouth close to his. She hesitated and he realised why. He had leaned backwards, away from her. She stayed there for long seconds and then started to move away. Javier caught her around the nape of her neck and dragged her back to him, intent on kissing her, and faltered again.

His gaze fell to her mouth.

He wanted to kiss her. His blood burned with the need until it bordered on controlling him but couldn't bring himself to go through with it. To kiss her would be to violate her. Not the bond with her master, but her purity. Just the thought of her soft mouth on his made him feel like a beast. If he kissed her, he wasn't sure he could retain control.

"What's wrong?" she whispered and he heard the hurt in her voice, saw it in her beautiful golden eyes when his leapt to them.

Her eyebrows furrowed and she touched his cheek, fingertips burning his flesh, the scent of her blood filling his senses.

His fangs dropped, pressing against his lips. He saw in her eyes the moment his changed, bloodlust swamping his irises and turning his pupils elliptical.

He raised a trembling hand and ran his thumb across her lower lip, and even that small caress was almost too much for him, branding her name on his soul.

"I want to kiss you," he uttered and her eyes dropped to his mouth. "Would you let a monster like me ruin you?"

She leaned closer again, her eyes locked on his, and his lips parted. "I don't see a monster anywhere. I only see a man... a man I want to kiss and make love with again... a beautiful man who ruined himself for me."

Javier closed his eyes at the first brush of her lips and tried to hold back, tried to keep still so he wouldn't cut her.

Her warm lips swept over his, teasing him into responding, lightening his insides and chasing his fears away.

She accepted him with a kiss, with words that moved his heart and tore down the walls of his restraint. He leaned into her, lifting his head, and kissed her, careful to keep his fangs away from her.

For all her beautiful words, she would probably curse him if he cut her. The taste of her blood would overwhelm him.

Lilah's tongue caressed his lower lip, coming dangerously close to his fangs. He told himself to pull away but he couldn't. She tamed the desire with a careful sweep of her tongue over their points. He stilled, barely breathing, letting her explore them with her tongue and probe his mouth, afraid that he might hurt her.

She curled her tongue and caressed the back of one fang, sending a shiver tripping through him.

He couldn't take any more.

He caught her shoulders and gently pushed her away, his breathing laboured, fingers tight against her soft flesh as he fought for control.

"Too much?" she said and he nodded, closed his eyes and hung his head forwards. She surprised him by running her hand over his hair, combing the light brown lengths back so gently that it soothed the raging hunger inside him, giving him back control over himself and his need for her. "I'll be more careful next time."

Next time? He groaned at the thought. If she dared do that again, he would bite her. It had taken every ounce of his will to resist her this time. Next time it wouldn't be enough.

Lilah rose to her feet, held her hand out to him, and smiled. "We can shower later."

Javier frowned.

Later?

He wasn't going to argue with her, not when she looked so seductive and tempting standing over him, affording him a glorious view up the short skirt of her black dress. Devil, he hungered to place his hand on the inside of her knee and slide it up past the top of her black socks to the creamy soft skin of her inner thigh.

He wanted to sink his teeth into that warm flesh and hear her moan his name as he drank from her vein. He wanted to be a beast with her.

She looked around the room, her gaze pausing on something, and then back down at him.

"We should tie you up to make sure it's clear I initiated things."

Javier stared at her, feeling a little lost and as though he had just imagined her saying something so wicked and arousing. She wanted to tie him up. Was she expecting someone to barge in on them or was she just using that as an excuse?

It made one thing clear to him. Neither of them could muster the fear of the law they should feel. She intoxicated him too much with each glance, smile and soft caress, for him to care that right now her master was probably heading here to the theatre.

He had never been one to run from his enemies and he wasn't going to start now. It didn't matter where they were. Her master would find her. If he ran with her, he would only be making things worse for her. If he stayed here and waited for Lord Ashville to come, he could spare her punishment. He would take responsibility for his actions.

But he wouldn't take it lying down.

Lilah crossed the room to his king-size four-poster bed and his clothes strewn across the midnight blue covers.

She wasn't under her master's command. His touch didn't pain her and she wanted him as much as he needed her. Her bond with Lord Ashville was incomplete.

When Lord Ashville came for him, he would face him.

Lilah picked up his dark silver-grey silk tie and his belt and turned towards him, a wicked smile on her angelic face.

And he would fight him for her.

CHAPTER 5

Javier rose to his feet, locked the door, and crossed the room to Lilah. She blushed a dark tempting shade of red and held up the tie and belt. The nervous edge to her golden eyes and her scent betrayed her but she didn't back down.

She glanced at the midnight blue silk covers on his bed and Javier obeyed, unable to resist her when she looked so seductive and tempting.

He knelt on the bed, crawled into the centre of it, and lay with his head on the feather pillows. The bedclothes were cool beneath him. He closed his eyes, focused so his fangs went away and his eyes changed back, and then looked at her. He raised his hands above his head, placing his wrists close to the carved mahogany headboard, and waited for her.

Lilah didn't hesitate. She bravely mounted the bed, looked at the elaborate design on the headboard, and frowned. He knew what the problem was. There wasn't much in the way of places she could tie him to and even if he stretched his arms out, the tie and belt wouldn't be long enough to secure him to the posts.

He held his hand up, got onto his knees and looked for a weak point in the carved design. Lilah gasped as he punched one hole and then another close to it. He shook his hand, splattering the sheets with blood, and then raised his knuckles to his mouth and licked them.

"That doesn't exactly make it look as though I forced you into this." She frowned at him as he turned towards her and then it melted away when she saw his hand.

She took hold of it and he could only stare as she raised it to her lips and kissed his knuckles.

The sight of his blood on her lips was too much for him to bear.

He swooped on them, moaning as he claimed her mouth and tasted his blood.

She bent backwards, her hands against his upper arms, clutching him so tightly that he felt her nails digging into his flesh. He groaned again, aroused by the hint of pain, the scent of blood, and the thought of her tying him up.

Lilah pushed him backwards and knelt before him, her breasts threatening to spill out of her dress with each hard breath she drew. Her outfit played havoc with his libido, especially when she leaned towards him, her cleavage on display, and pressed her hand into his shoulder and gave it a shove.

Javier fell backwards onto the bed, staring up at her, a willing slave. He obediently raised his hands to the headboard again, eager to feel the silk and leather against his wrists, binding him. Hungry to be at her mercy.

She tied his right wrist first with the silk tie and it was too soft against his skin. He wanted to feel the bite of it, to feel as though he was powerless.

"Tighter," he whispered and she blushed again, cheeks blazing, but did as he said.

She untied it and tugged it tighter, until it squeezed his wrist and tore a groan from him.

He nodded when she looked concerned. He could take it.

When she tied his left wrist with his Italian leather belt, she did it up so tightly that it pinched his skin and squeezed his bones.

Lilah moved towards him until her thighs were eye level with him and he could smell himself on her, smell their combined arousal.

His cock twitched against the black towel, hungry to be inside her again, to climax this time, uncaring of the law. She was his. He would make Lord Ashville recognise that.

When she moved to kneel close to his face and reached over the back of the headboard, he couldn't tear his eyes away from her thighs. He stared at them as she fumbled with the tie and the belt, trying to knot them together, tugging his hands forwards so they pressed against the headboard, the splintered wood rough on his wrists.

She looked pleased with herself when she sat back.

"You know these can't really hold me," he said playfully and she scolded him with a frown.

"It's not as though we have real shackles." Her frown didn't shift. "You'll have to play along."

"I know where to get some." He smiled up at her. "Knock on Snow's door and ask to borrow his."

Her face blanched. His smile widened.

"Do you really think I would let you wander off to see Snow?" His humour died at the thought. Snow was unpredictable. Dangerous. He couldn't be trusted around anyone, not even his brother Antoine. "It was a bad joke. Maybe we can get some real ones if I make it through this."

Tears sparkled on her lashes and her shoulders sagged. "Don't speak like that. He can't do anything to you now. I made you do this."

She honestly believed that. It was so sweet of her, so beautiful that she had fooled herself into believing with all of her heart that this made any difference.

He nodded, not wanting to see her cry because of him and her fear of what lay ahead for both of them. He would play along just as she had asked and would pretend with her so his heart stopped aching and the tears in her eyes went away. He didn't want this time with her to be full of sorrow.

He wanted it to be full of love.

He wanted to find Heaven with her before he faced Hell.

Lilah swallowed, rubbed the heel of her hands across her eyes, and drew a long deep breath. Her forced smile didn't fool him.

"Come here." Javier nodded his head, indicating where he wanted her.

She leaned over him, settling her hands on his bare chest, and pressed her lips to his.

Her soft kiss warmed him, erasing the hurt and fear growing inside him, replacing it with hunger and love.

He held the words back, afraid they would be too much for her to handle and she would break under the weight of them when everything between them was so uncertain.

When everything was over and she finally belonged to him, he would tell her that he was in love with her and that he wanted her to be his forever.

Lilah kissed away from his mouth, down to his chin and then along his jaw. He wanted to take hold of her and bring her mouth back to his but the tug of restraints around his wrists reminded him that he was powerless to do as he pleased.

Lilah was in control now.

He had never surrendered control to anyone before. It had always seemed like too great a risk to him. In the few seconds it would take him to break free, whoever he was with could stake and kill him.

Her hand came to rest on the point over his heart and Javier realised that he trusted Lilah. Implicitly. He knew in his heart that he was safe with her and that she would never hurt him.

And he knew that she trusted him too.

She had let him kiss her when his fangs had been out and had kissed him when she'd had his blood on her lips, both times when he could have easily acted on his lust for her blood.

The thought of biting her had his fangs descending again. Lilah paused and he felt her eyes on his mouth. She straddled his waist and leaned over him, her gaze boring into his lips. Her soft fingertips against his lower lip were a command he obeyed, parting them for her and letting her see his fangs.

The beautiful look of fascination on her face as she carefully ran a fingertip over one of his canines stole his ability to breathe and he waited, wanting to see what she would do.

She turned her hand so her palm faced him and pressed the pad of her index finger against the point of his fang, and flinched.

The coppery aroma of her blood filled his nostrils and then the sweet fragrance of it flooded his mouth.

His eyes changed again and he lurched upwards, every muscle tensing, ravenous for a taste of her.

She didn't shy away or flee as he expected.

She bravely remained seated astride him and turned her hand again, so the tiny bead of blood on the tip of her finger touched his tongue.

The flavour of her exploded in his mouth and his cock strained against the tight confines of the towel.

He bucked his hips, aching for some relief, so hard that it hurt, and sucked her finger. His low guttural groan tore a gasp from her and he tugged at his restraints, hungry to drag her down to him and have her.

"Javier," she whispered and the sound of his name spoken so reverently by her broke through the haze of his bloodlust and sent him crashing back to reality.

He opened his eyes and stared into hers, her finger still held fast in his mouth.

"You can bite me if you desire it."

How could she speak to him so openly and with such respect when she couldn't speak of her master like it? It made him feel as though she was already his, and that was dangerous.

Javier released her finger and she took it back. He shook his head and a touch of hurt laced her expression. He wanted to reach up and touch her face when she looked like that, needed to smooth away her pain and make it all better.

"Not yet," he whispered, his fangs sharp against his tongue.

He had meant to say never, that he would never use her like that to satisfy his thirst for blood and she meant more to him than just a source of sustenance to bring his darker side under control.

Not yet.

He wanted to bite her but feared it.

His touch didn't hurt her for some reason but he didn't know whether his bite would. He had heard that biting an owned human caused them excruciating pain, almost triple that of a touch.

He couldn't risk that.

"When all this is over?" she said, as though she had read the desire in his heart again.

Did she know him so well that she could see through him and into his soul? Were they tied there, one in heart and soul, joined by their feelings?

He nodded. "When you are mine."

"I want to be yours."

Javier rolled his eyes closed, his heart singing sweet mercy.

She wanted to be his.

Lilah grazed her hands over his chest and then up his arms to his wrists. She held them and leaned over him, pressing her forehead and nose against his.

"And you will be mine," she whispered and he shivered and groaned.

"Forever." He said it without thinking and instantly stilled, waiting for her to scoot away and fear him.

She hated her master because he had bonded with her against her will. He feared she would hate him too for wanting to make her belong to him instead.

"Forever." That word breathed against his lips pained him, but even if forever was only this night it would be enough for him. "For a man tied up, you're thinking too much."

Lilah kissed along his jaw, shifting her body down his at the same time, and he groaned his agreement when the apex of her thighs brushed his groin, stirring him back into hardness.

He tugged at his restraints again and focused on the fact she had him tied up and at her mercy, and what she was doing to him. She licked the left side of his neck and lightly bit him.

Javier bucked on instinct, a flash of hunger burning up his blood and a deep groan escaping his lips.

Lilah giggled and bit again, harder this time, and he snarled.

She stilled, her rapid pulse pounding in his mind, the feel of her heart hammering against his chest pushing at his control.

"Gentler." Javier forced the word out from between clenched teeth, his fangs cutting into his gums.

He feared she would stop completely.

Lilah moved and chased that fear and all reason from his mind by nibbling along his collarbone. She pinned his shoulders to the bed and licked his throat again, tracing up the jugular, and nipped his earlobe. Javier fought to retain control. She lowered her mouth again and bit the curve of his throat.

His blood turned to liquid fire that ignited every inch of him, his balls tightened and his cock quivered a second before the world exploded in bright sparks that burned wherever she touched him, fiercest where her teeth pressed into his flesh.

"Ay, Dios, Lilah," Javier breathed and relaxed into the bed, his length still twitching.

He let his hands hang from the restraints, trying to gather himself and trying not to feel ashamed about what had just happened.

He waited for her to laugh or say something that would crush what little male pride he had left.

She drew back and stared down at him, her pupils wide and dark with arousal. "If a vampire bit you, would you have done this with them?"

He shook his head.

No.

It was Lilah's teeth on him that had lit the touch paper and caused him to detonate.

"If I had fangs..." she caressed a line down his throat with her fingertip and then leaned over and replaced it with her tongue, sweeping the soft wet tip of it over the point where she had bitten and sent him crashing over the edge. It tickled his sensitised flesh, sending ripples of echoes of his orgasm through him, "and I bit you... would you come then too?"

"Cristo... just the thought of you doing that... Lilah." His cock stiffened again, hard and aching for more.

He wanted her to bite him, wanted her fangs in his throat and his blood flowing into her.

He wanted to be the one to give her those fangs, to bring her into his world as his mate.

She raised herself, drawing her body away from his, and slid her hand down over his stomach to his hard shaft. He groaned as she cupped him through the damp towel, squeezing and teasing him.

"Lilah," he whispered and couldn't get the rest of what he had wanted to say out.

He wanted to beg her to touch him, to take him inside her again and ride him, to place her mouth on him and suck him.

He wanted it all.

She moved downwards, kissing his chest and swirling her tongue around his left nipple. He arched against her, ticklish from his orgasm, and moaned at the feel of her nails raking down his stomach. She shifted one knee between his thighs and her hands left him.

Javier looked down the length of his body at her, his temperature soaring at the sight of her in the short black dress, her breasts on the brink of tumbling out as she leaned over him with her backside in the air.

He growled, wanting to be behind her, knocking her knees apart and sinking his body into her wet warmth.

Her wicked smile stole his heart.

She tugged the waist of his towel and opened it, revealing his cock. Her gaze fell to it and she ran her fingers down the rigid length to his balls and cupped them. She hesitated then, as though she couldn't decide or wasn't sure what to do next.

He wanted to tell her to do whatever she wanted with him. He was hers to command, to do as she pleased with and use in her search for pleasure.

He lay and watched her as she lowered her mouth to his erection and ran her tongue up the length of it. She swirled it around the blunt head, moaning so low that his cock jumped eagerly. She smiled and licked him again, torturing him this time with the bare tip of her tongue. It wasn't enough. He lifted his hips and she pressed them down, pinning them to the bed. He groaned, thrilled by the feel of her restraining him, controlling him.

She sat back, reached around her, and unzipped her dress.

Javier swallowed and stared, hungry for his first glimpse of her bare body. She teased him, slowly removing her dress, making sure she kept as much of her hidden from him as possible by keeping the dress in front of her.

He growled again and her heart remained steady this time, no trace of fear entering her blood.

She was growing used to him.

Did she trust the darker side of him now?

He would never hurt her. He might snarl and growl and snap but it was only because she drove him wild and made him burn for her with a need that consumed him.

He bit his lip and clenched his fists when she finally lowered the dress, revealing the curve of her breasts at first and then the lacy trim on the cups of her black bra. Another growl escaped him as the rest of her bra came into view and then the flat plane of her stomach and finally she moved the dress aside, tossing it onto the floor and leaving herself on display.

He wanted her bra gone too, and her panties.

He wanted to tear them off her with his fangs and devour her nipples and plunge his tongue into her core to taste her.

"Come to me," he whispered, aching to taste her on his tongue.

She shook her head and smiled.

Vixen.

She reached around behind her, undid her bra, and drew it down her arms. The first peek of her dusky pink nipples over the cups of her bra did him in. His cock throbbed and he bucked his hips, desperate for her to touch him.

She did.

She let her bra fall onto the bed, leaned over him, and ran her breasts over his hard length. He groaned, rolled his eyes closed and tipped his head into the pillow.

It was too much.

He tugged, tempted to break the restraints, torn between remaining at her mercy and seizing control.

Lilah placed his cock between her breasts and held them, squeezing him between them and moving up and down.

The box flashed across his closed eyes, the thrill of easing into her for the first time while she watched the performance returning full force and carrying him away.

He had never done anything so erotic and so wicked.

Slowly entering her as the man on stage had penetrated the woman, feeling Lilah shiver and tense around him, her warm wetness enveloping him, had brought him dangerously close to coming. He'd had to stop and wait until the hunger had receded before continuing, and even then it had been difficult to hold off his climax until Lilah had found hers.

He wanted to come inside her this time.

Needed to claim her fully.

Javier opened his eyes to find she had moved up him while he had been reliving their first time together. She leaned over him, her hands on the top of the headboard and her breasts dangling above him.

He craned his neck and captured her left nipple between his lips, and sucked it into his mouth. Her breathy moan tore a groan from him and he closed his eyes and suckled, rolling the hard bead between his teeth and fighting the temptation to nick it with his fangs and truly taste her.

She lifted away from him and he reached for her, craning his neck as much as possible and desperately trying to capture her nipple with the tip of his tongue.

He managed to flick it and she moaned so sweetly that he tried harder, ignoring how the bonds cut into his wrists and the splintered wood of his headboard stabbed into the back of his hands.

She lowered enough that he could sweep his tongue over her nipple again and then enough that he could suck it back into his mouth, harder this time. He wanted her wild with need, as hungry as he felt inside. He tipped his head to one side and looked down at her black knickers.

He needed to taste her.

"Come to me," he whispered and flicked her pert nipple with his tongue, hoping to tease her into doing as he asked this time. "I want to taste you on my tongue."

She blushed but didn't do as he said. She had reacted as sweetly when he had asked whether she enjoyed watching the couples fucking. Did she like to hear him speak so obscenely to her and be blunt about things?

"Let me fuck you with my tongue," he said in a rough commanding tone and she bit her lip and moaned, her blush deepening.

It worked.

She slipped out of her panties, revealing the soft neat thatch of dark curls at the apex of her thighs.

The scent of her drove him deeper into his hunger and his mouth watered, eager for the taste of her on his lips. He wanted to drink from her, to taste the nectar of her desire and know it flowed because of him. She wanted this as much as he did.

"Come to me, Lilah," he growled. "I must have you."

She nodded and then looked uncertain.

With his hands tied above his head, it would be difficult to get to her, but asking her to undo the makeshift cuffs wasn't going to get him anywhere. She would refuse and he didn't want her to take them off him anyway. He wanted her to pleasure herself on him, to be the one in control, and he wanted to hear her say what she was going to do to him.

"What do you want to do?" he whispered and her expression turned hesitant again. "Tell me, Lilah. I want to hear it. Don't be afraid. Do you know what I want to do to you?"

She shook her head, causing strands of her chestnut hair to fall out of her bun and brush her cheek. She hooked them behind her ears.

"I want to lick you until you scream my name, and then I want to bend you over and thrust my hard cock into you and make you scream again. I want to feel you come on me and know it was because of me... because you want me too." Javier was surprised he had managed to get everything out without stuttering or stumbling along the way. He had never been one for dirty talk but Lilah's reactions to it made him want to try it for the first time, intoxicated him and lured him into putting voice to his wicked thoughts so he could get another fix of her blush and the hunger that flashed in her eyes whenever she heard how much he desired her. "What do you want to do to me?"

She swallowed, mumbled something he didn't catch, and then bit her lip.

"Tell me, Lilah. Tell me what you want to do with me now you have me at your mercy."

Her gaze rose, locked on his, and she didn't hesitate this time. "I want to sit on your face and suck your cock until you can't take any more and then I want to... fuck you... until you come in me. I want you to come in me this time."

Devil, that was the most erotic thing anyone had ever said to him. His cock pulsed at the thought, hard and aching, telling him to make her skip the sucking and licking bit and jump right to the fucking.

Not fucking.

She could use that word and so could he, but this was beyond such a base sounding act.

No matter how they did it, it would be making love to him, joining them as one body, seeking pleasure in their desire and feelings for each other.

"Come to me then and let me taste your desire."

CHAPTER 6

Lilah wasn't getting used to hearing Javier speak to her like that.

Whenever he husked such dirty things, detailing what he wanted to do to her and telling her what to do, she blushed beetroot red and wasn't sure how to respond.

Saying what she had wanted to do to him empowered her though.

His reaction had been delicious, his hard cock leaping for her attention and his pupils swamping the colour in his irises and turning his gaze dark and hungry.

He liked to hear it and she thought he liked to hear that he was at her mercy too. The more things she said to him and him to her, the more comfortable and confident she felt.

She ran her hand over his erection, still amazed that she had made him come by merely biting him, and what she had said to him afterwards.

Did she want to be a vampire? If Javier wanted to make her into one, would she consent to it so she could be with him forever?

The thought of it was strangely appealing, exciting, and her heart was willing to take the leap and trust that the forever he had spoken of was something he truly wanted with her.

"Lilah, you torture me," he whispered, hoarse and rough, Spanish accented voice thick with desire. Her eyes widened when she realised she had taken to stroking his cock, her fingers curled around it, and he was thrusting through the ring of them. "Come to me."

She nodded and he groaned and didn't stop as she moved into position on him, seating herself above his face with her mouth near his hungry cock. She teased him first, holding his shaft and licking the crown, running her tongue over it and tasting the salty tang of his seed.

He moaned, his cool breath tickling her pussy, luring her into wanting to lower herself onto his face and giving him the taste of her that he desired.

"Please, Lilah," he said and the moment she dropped her hips closer to him, his tongue delved into her plush petals and found her clit.

Lilah groaned loudly and then stifled herself by wrapping her mouth around his cock and sucking it. The more she sucked and licked him, shifting her hand up and down his hard length, the more pleasure he gave her.

He moaned into her, swirling his tongue around her sensitive clit and then licking upwards. She breathed hard against his cock as he thrust it into her mouth and thrust his tongue into her slick core at the same time. His groan was nothing short of profane and erotic, full of deep satisfaction that echoed within her.

She sucked him harder, eager for the taste of him again, desperate to make him continue alternating between plunging his stiff tongue into her wet sheath and suckling her clit.

He lowered his mouth and swirled his tongue around her aroused nub and it was too much for her. She shifted her hips up, out of his reach, and breathed hard against him, struggling to hold back. She didn't want to climax. Not yet.

She crawled away from him and he growled again, the threatening sound of it sending a chill chasing over her skin and down her spine. She was coming to like it when he growled at her, marking the difference between them in such a primal way. He was a vampire. A powerful predator.

And she had him at her mercy.

Lilah paused and looked over her shoulder at him, seeing the need and desire in his eyes, the fierce hunger for her in the red tinge to his irises, and the hope buried beneath the surface, locked deep in his heart.

He felt something for her, and she felt something for him, and that meant that there was nothing wrong with what they were doing. She didn't care if vampire society said what was happening between them was forbidden.

She would fight them all so she could be with him.

She would fight for the man that she loved.

The hunger in his eyes softened, curiosity surfacing in them as he searched hers, as though he had seen the feelings she held in her heart.

Lilah turned to face him, straddling his hips, and stared into his eyes, letting him see that this meant something and that she would fight for it. She wouldn't let him suffer the consequences of their actions alone. She would stand by his side and tell the world that her master had no control over her and that she loved Javier with all of her heart, and she didn't care if that was wrong, because it felt right to her.

She reached behind her, gripped his cock, and held it poised at her entrance.

"Javier?" she whispered and the words fled her lips and her courage fell away.

He tugged at his restraints. She gasped when he snapped them, grabbed her upper arms and pulled her down to him. He kissed her and rolled her onto her back, his mouth fusing with hers, tongue plundering with fierce thrusts and sweeps. She groaned, buried her fingers into the longer lengths of his sandy brown hair and wrapped her legs around him as he plunged his cock hard into her.

His answering moan was low and deep, full of feral hunger that turned it into a snarl.

"Tell me what you were thinking," he uttered against her throat, kissing it and nibbling as he withdrew and thrust back into her, burying his body deep within hers, joining them as one. He caught one of her legs, getting his arm under her knee and holding it up. She groaned, unable to find her voice when he was driving her out of her head, his pelvis slamming against her clit with each deep plunge of his cock into her wet core. "Tell me, Lilah. Tell me I am not alone in this. Give me the strength to fight."

God.

She wanted to.

She wanted to cling to the hope that everything would turn out all right in the end just as he had said it would but she couldn't fool herself. She wrapped her arms around him and moaned as he moved slower and deeper, long thrusts of his cock that threatened to have her climaxing before she managed to put voice to her feelings and give him the reassurance he craved.

The thought that so strong a man needed her with such ferocity, that she could give him the strength that he sought with only a few honest words when he was so powerful in her eyes, awed and empowered her. It made her strong too.

"You're not alone, Javier," she whispered and his name came out as a long moan as he pumped her, thrusting his long cock into her, completing her in a way she had never felt before. She felt so connected to him, so strong but so weak at the same time. Her happiness, her pleasure, her future, all of it was in his hands and it scared her. They had given up their fight against their feelings but rather than giving them the joy it should have it had given them pain and fear. He kissed her throat, whispered low Spanish words against it, words that sounded so romantic and so full of love that they brought tears to her eyes. "I'm right here with you."

He growled and held her tighter, his fingertips digging into her thigh and her shoulder, his hips pumping harder and faster. Each deep plunge of his cock pushed her closer to the edge. Each brush of his pelvis against her aroused nub sent shivers chasing up her thighs and tore a moan from her throat.

She leaned her head back and to one side, sensing his intent, inviting him in and wanting him to go through with it this time.

She wasn't afraid of the consequences.

"Forgive me... I cannot help... I must." He snarled, withdrew sharply and then thrust his cock hard into her as he buried his fangs deep into her throat.

Lilah cried out, fire sweeping through every inch of her, burning her up as she trembled and quaked, her body throbbing hard with her orgasm.

Shivers and tingles cascaded over her skin, up and down her thighs in time with each pulse of his cock inside her and each pull he made on her blood.

She clutched him to her, unable to do anything else but ride out each tremor of bliss that rocked her, her breath stuttering and heart stammering in her chest.

Javier sucked softly on her neck, his hips making shallow thrusts, hands tightly gripping her.

No pain.

Only deep pleasure that sent her floating and drifting away, that slowly broke through the tremors of her orgasm and opened her mind to the feel of her blood flowing from her and into Javier.

With each drop he took from her, the horizon in her mind expanded, unravelling outwards, until it met his and merged.

She could feel him.

Was this what it was like to be bitten by a vampire and have them take blood from you?

She had never experienced it before.

Javier's thoughts were warm around her, soft as they encased her, and she felt as though they were holding her as surely as his hands were. She fell into them, unafraid, opening herself to him in the hope that he would know that she was there too and would feel her thoughts as she could feel his.

It was too difficult to tell him that she loved him right now when everything was so uncertain but she could let him feel it. The feeling inside her intensified and the warmth she felt increased, suffusing her and making her smile.

She didn't understand what was happening but she didn't need to in order to know Javier's feelings for her in the connection forged between their blood.

He withdrew his fangs and licked the puncture marks on her throat, softly and slowly, with infinite care. She was growing sleepy by the time he finally finished and placed a kiss on her throat.

"Sleep a while with me," he whispered into her ear and rolled them over, gathering her close to him. He tugged the bedclothes over her and around them both, and then wrapped his arms around her shoulders, holding her.

Lilah didn't want to sleep but the incredible warmth flowing through her and the feelings she could sense in Javier carried her away.

CHAPTER 7

Javier stared down at Lilah where she lay in his arms, her head resting against his forearm and her slow breaths skating warmly over his bare chest.

Each beat of her steady heart marked another passing second and brought him closer to the time when he would have to face her master. He refused to fear it while he held her safe in his arms, her nude body curled close to his and her right hand on his left shoulder, close to the place where she had bitten him.

It felt so peaceful that he could almost believe that this time with her would never end and they would drift through eternity like this, quiet and sated, alternating between sleeping and making love.

He drew his left hand away from her and carefully lifted the strands of her dark chestnut hair from her face, tucking them back into the loose mess of her bun.

She was so beautiful.

His Lilah.

He traced a lone fingertip down her warm satin cheek, unable to remember the last time he had felt so content and had watched over a woman as she slept in his arms.

Not this past century at least.

The theatre had become his life since the night it opened, stealing all his time and energy.

Until Lilah had walked into his life and filled it with new colours and sounds, and scents, and rekindled his desire to live.

Her nose wrinkled as he brushed it and she frowned, buried her head into the crook of his arm, and curled up.

Javier smiled.

He loved her so much.

He bent his head to press a kiss to her brow and she rolled away from him and wriggled backwards until her bottom pressed into his hip. The heat of her against him and the sight of her peachy backside so close to his crotch shattered the peace and stoked the fire of passion back into life within him.

His cock twitched and started to harden, and he rolled onto his side and nestled it in the crack of her bottom. She moaned in her sleep and rubbed against him, tearing a low groan from his throat in response.

Javier dropped kisses on the back of her shoulder, the nape of her neck, and then the top of her shoulder close to where he had bitten her.

Bitten her.

He smiled and kissed the marks, glad that he hadn't hurt her with his bite.

It was further proof to him that Lord Ashville's bond to her was incomplete. It boosted his hope that the law would land on his side when time came to face her so-called master. The sacred law spoke of a vampire violating it and that the pain caused to the human would mark the violation.

Lilah was right.

It didn't speak of a human violating the law or that the owned human would feel no pain. He needed to speak to Antoine about it as soon as possible and see what he made of the situation.

Antoine would be angry with him for violating it in the first place since he hadn't known then that his touch and bite wouldn't pain Lilah, but his old friend had to see that this case was unique and required those who ruled the vampires to decide on the outcome.

Antoine couldn't let Lord Ashville act out the penalty without an investigation into the bond between him and Lilah.

Javier wrapped his arm around her stomach and pulled her roughly against him, grinding his hard cock against the crack of her backside at the same time.

He pressed his mouth to her shoulder, breathing in the trace of her blood scent and closing his eyes.

He should go to Antoine now but he couldn't muster the strength to leave the bed and Lilah's side yet, not until he had seen pleasure on her face one more time and seen in her eyes that she shared his feelings.

"Lilah," he whispered and kissed along her neck, up the delicate slope of it to her ear. "Are you awake?"

She moaned and rubbed her bottom against him. "One of us certainly is."

He smiled. "It is still night. I am supposed to be awake... and so are you."

Lilah sighed and rolled to face him, throwing her knee over his hip. Her mound pressed against his erection, heating it and bringing back memories of how tight and hot she was. He groaned.

"How long was I asleep?" she muttered.

"Only an hour." He smiled down at her when her eyes fluttered open and her beautiful golden irises rose to meet his.

Lilah frowned. "What were you doing in that time?"

"Watching you sleep." His honest answer drew a harder frown from her. He pressed the pad of his thumb between her eyes and smoothed it away, still smiling ear to ear at her. "You are beautiful when you are sleeping in my arms."

She smiled and snuggled closer to him. "Am I not beautiful any other time?"

"All the time," he whispered and kissed her. She opened to him, tipping her head back and willingly accepting his kiss.

He closed his eyes in pleasure, lost in the feel of her mouth on his, so warm and soft and sweet, everything he had ever dreamed of experiencing. She honestly didn't think he was a monster. He had growled, snarled, broken his bonds and bitten her, and she had accepted all of it.

All of him.

"Mmm," she hummed and drew away from him again. Her fingers stroked the left side of his neck, her eyes tracking them from the point below his earlobe to his collarbone. "Where did you get this?"

"In a fight." There was no point in masking who he was and the things he had done.

She would find out and he preferred that she knew such things about him sooner rather than later. He wanted her to base her decision to be with him on all the facts, with her eyes open to what he was and his past.

"Are you a good fighter?" Her gaze met his, inquisitive but soft and full of acceptance. Her steady heart told him that she wasn't afraid of his answer or whatever he might tell her. She already knew what he was.

He nodded. "Better than the man who gave me this, anyway."

"What happened to him?"

He didn't hesitate. "I killed him."

"Was he human or vampire?"

She was certainly awake now, her golden irises bright with curiosity. He stroked her cheek, swept strands of her dark hair from her face, revealing it to him so he could drink his fill of it.

"Vampire hunter," he said and then added, "I have killed my share of hunters, and vampires... and humans. There were times when I was younger when it was more difficult to control my hunger. It is something all vampires go through during their first two centuries."

She smiled. "You say that as though it's a mere handful of years. It's twice the age within my grasp."

His face fell and so did hers when he touched her cheek again, staring into her eyes. "Would you want to live that long, Lilah?"

She dropped her gaze to his chest and traced patterns on his pectorals, sending shivers of need spiralling down through him to his groin. She didn't even seem to notice that she was torturing him with her touch, teasing him towards the brink of despair and losing control.

He wanted her again, hungered to feel her under his fingers and be inside her once more.

She was making it difficult for him to remain talking and he knew that it was important to her.

"Perhaps. Would I have to become a vampire to live for centuries?" That question came out sounding like one she had considered many times but had never had the courage to seek the answer to it.

"Not necessarily. Regular intake of blood from a vampire you are bonded with could grant you a very long life... but it would only slow your aging. By the time you reached two centuries, you would likely be very old and grey and tired of life." Javier didn't want that for her. He wanted her to remain as she was now, beautiful and youthful, and his. He hesitated, toying with a strand of her hair, and watched his fingers, not brave enough to look her in the eye when he found the courage to say what he needed to. "If you wanted to live as long as I have and remain as you are, you would have to become a vampire. Would you ever consent to becoming a vampire, Lilah?"

Her fingers stilled against his chest and her heart skipped a beat, giving her away. Whatever she said, he knew the answer that she held deep in her soul. She was afraid of becoming a vampire.

"I thought vampires didn't like to turn people and taint their bloodline?"

Javier smiled again. "Some think that way. Mainly the aristocrats. Keeping their families pure has become a sort of mission to them."

"You're an elite, aren't you?"

He nodded against the deep blue pillow and she looked up at him, right into his eyes. There was a spark of warmth in hers, something akin to affection, and an urge to ask her what she was thinking gripped him again but he let it fall away instead and answered her question.

"Yes, I am elite. That means my family has human blood in it. I wasn't turned, but my father turned my mother, and they had me, my younger brother and my sister. They still live in Spain. My sister recently married the man she turned."

"Is that where you went?"

Javier nodded again. "I missed you when I was there. Watching my sister marry and seeing my parents again... I kept thinking about you."

Her eyes widened and he wasn't sure what to say.

Had he given himself away?

He should have been more guarded with what he had said but the words had flowed out of him so naturally that he hadn't thought to censor them.

If she knew that he wanted that for them, he wanted the fairytale of turning her and then marrying her before his family, then he was glad in a way. It would give her time to consider it without the pressure of him asking outright.

"Did you miss me?" he whispered, trying to give her something to respond to so she didn't feel as though she had to say anything about him turning her.

"Not at all." She looked deadly serious, so much so that his heart dropped into his stomach. She pushed him onto his back and climbed astride him, pressing her warmth against his cock, teasing it back into hardness. She smiled at last, leaned over so her stomach and chest pressed against his, and kissed his chin. "I missed you like crazy... especially when Callum mentioned you would be away for a whole month. That must have been some wedding celebration."

Javier shrugged, settled his hands on her bare backside, and shifted her upwards so he could reach her mouth and kiss her.

If he married her, the celebrations would last longer than a month.

He would be celebrating it forever.

He kissed her slowly, hoping to stop her questions, but she broke away from him and looked down into his eyes.

"How old are your brother and sister?"

He knew where this was heading. "My sister is three hundred and fifty seven... eight even. My brother is five hundred and two. I was away for a month shortly after you first arrived because of his five hundredth birthday. I am six hundred and thirty three."

"I'm that transparent?" Her rosy lips curved back into a soft smile and he couldn't resist kissing her again. She settled her elbows on the pillows above his shoulders and returned the kiss this time, her mouth playing gently against his, tongue barely touching his as they met and parted. She drew back again. "So you're just the six hundred years older than me?"

Javier palmed her buttocks. "Does that make me too old for you?"

She peppered kisses on his lips and cheek and then his jaw. "Not at all. Does that mean you're strong? I heard that vampires over five hundred were much stronger... but that elite vampires aren't as strong as aristocrats."

Javier abruptly wrapped his arms around her and held her head against his chest. "Do not think about it. I will take care of it... just... everything will be alright."

She nodded against him and he clutched her shoulders and raised her off him, so he could see her face. There was worry in her golden eyes, fear that he could smell in her blood. He sighed and cupped her cheek, holding her gaze.

"Maybe I need to take your mind off it." Javier raised his hips beneath her, pressing his erection into her warmth.

Her saucy smile stole his heart.

Lilah wriggled against him, pressed her hands against his chest and pushed herself up.

Javier groaned at the sight of her firm round breasts and covered them with his hands, feeling the heat of her against his palms. Her eyelids drooped when he thumbed her nipples, circling them at first before pinching and rolling them between his index finger and thumb.

She tipped her head back and moaned, a goddess above him, beautifully bare and enticing.

Javier lowered one hand from her breasts, skimming it down over the smooth plane of her stomach to her hip, and then following the curve of her thigh downwards. He turned his hand and slid it beneath her, parting her and seeking her aroused nub.

She lifted off him, her gasp cutting the silence, and he watched her face as he touched her, drank in her pleasure as it rippled across her features, causing her eyebrows to knit one moment and then shoot upwards the next.

Her eyes opened and she looked down at him, her body shifting against his hand, hips rotating in the most sensual way he had ever seen. He wanted her to move that way on him, to swirl her hips around as he pumped into her and brought her to climax.

He eased his hand forwards and slowly sank two fingers into her warm heat. She gasped and moaned his name in a way that he had been dying to hear again. It sounded so sexy and hungry when she growled it like that, her voice rough with desire and need. It was a command, an order for him to keep going and give her the pleasure she sought with him.

Javier obeyed.

He pumped her slowly with one hand, pressing his fingers into the softness of her core to give her more pleasure, and teased her nipple with his other hand. She moved faster, thrusting down onto his fingers, riding them.

"More, Javier," she uttered and he groaned, his cock bobbing at the command in her tone.

He would give her more. He would give her so much that she screamed his name when she came this time.

Javier slid his fingers free of her.

She opened her eyes and he killed her protest before it reached her lips by positioning his hard length beneath her and easing her back onto it. Her words came out as a low moan instead as she sank back onto his cock and he joined her, groaning as her tight sheath enveloped him.

He was never getting used to the feel of her around him, so hot and wet, gripping his cock in a way that made him want to stay inside her forever.

Lilah pressed her hands against his hips, raised herself up on his cock and then sank back down again, pushing him deeper this time.

He groaned and grasped her hips.

She smiled, held his gaze, and placed her hands over his as she started to move on him, her breasts bouncing and swaying with each swirl of her hips.

"Lilah," he whispered, lost in her eyes and the feel of her riding his cock, rotating her hips so it circled inside her, buried deep in her hot core.

At this rate, he was going to be the one screaming her name as he came.

She smiled wickedly, tipped her head back and opened her mouth in a sigh.

So wanton.

He couldn't get enough of watching her as she sought her pleasure, doing as she wanted, using him to satisfy her desire. She whirled her hips with each thrust of his cock into her, driving him out of his mind until all he could do was surrender to his instincts.

He tensed his backside with each of her down thrusts, pumping his cock up into her, short frenzied thrusts that tore groans from her throat and made her clutch his hands, her fingers pressing into his.

"Javier," she moaned and the sound of it drove him on, fuelling his need for her. He clasped her hips and moved her on him, roughening the thrusts, bringing her down hard on his cock. She arched her back and he choked out a groan at the tightness of her around him. Her answering moan was louder this time. "Javier."

He snarled and gave her what she wanted, his hips pumping hard, plunging his cock into her maddening heat and surrendering to his urge to have her.

She moaned a little higher with each deep thrust of his hard length that sent her breasts bobbing and body quivering. Her teeth sank into her lower lip, the sight of them teasing it too much for him to handle.

His fangs extended, hunger for her blood flooding his veins and swamping his senses. His eyes switched next, bringing the low lit bedroom into sharp bright focus. His heightened senses made everything feel a thousand times better and a million times too good for him to handle.

Lilah rode him with frenzied thrusts, her hands claiming her breasts, the sight of her pushing him over the edge.

He lifted her off him, ignoring her mewls, and set her down on the bed on her front. She moaned when he moved behind her and lifted her onto her hands and knees, and then cried out his name when he plunged his hard cock back into her wet core. She rocked forwards with each hard thrust of his body into hers and he growled as she tightened around him, her mewls and moans filling the room.

Javier grasped her hips, pumping her hard and fast, losing himself in the heat of the moment and desperately trying to hold himself back so he didn't hurt her.

He nudged her knees further apart and roughened his thrusts.

The feel of his balls hitting her pussy with each plunge of his cock into her, the sound of her moaning his name each time the head of his length struck deep inside her, and the scent of her arousal and blood all combined to tip him over the edge.

"Javier!" Lilah's shout of bliss and the tremble of her warm body around his aching cock was the final straw.

With a hoarse snarl, Javier slammed his body hard and deep into hers and held himself there as he came, his cock quivering and pulsing discordantly to her body.

He clutched her to him, holding her so she couldn't pull away from him, needing to catch his breath and make the most of being inside her. She sighed when he bent forwards, resting his forehead against her sweat soaked back. The thundering rush of her heart beat in his mind and the scent of her blood filled his nostrils.

Javier licked her back, tasting her salty skin, savouring it as much as he was being inside her. He closed his eyes and reluctantly released her. She didn't move away from him. She stayed with his softening cock inside her, trembling beneath him, her breathing fast and hard.

"Did I hurt you?" he whispered and kissed her back, wanting to soothe away her pain with his touch if he had.

"No." She pushed herself up, so he had to rise with her, and knelt before him, her back against his front. She reached over behind her and ran her hand through his hair. He loved the heat of her body against his. The giggle that escaped her was music to his ears. "I just need a moment for the room to stop spinning."

He smiled and pressed kisses to her shoulder, relieved that he hadn't gone too far. It was hard to keep control when he was inside her.

Javier withdrew from her, turned her in his arms and lay her back down on the bed.

He lay next to her, covered her with the blanket, and held her close to him, waiting for her to fall asleep again. It didn't take long for her breathing to turn soft and slow and her heartbeat to settle, telling him that she had drifted off.

He didn't want to scare her by leaving her alone while she was awake and he had to see Antoine. The temptation to remain with her was overwhelming but he fought it. He would lock the door to his apartment and would find Antoine as quickly as possible and return before she woke.

He waited a few minutes longer, struggling to convince himself to leave, telling himself that he had to be sure that she was asleep before he moved.

With a sigh, he gently lifted her head, pulled his arm out from beneath her, and laid it back down on the dark blue pillow. He pressed a soft kiss to her lips, covered her with the blanket, and slipped from the bed.

Javier had put his black boxers and his tailored trousers on before he remembered that they had used his belt as a restraint. He glanced across at the bed.

It wasn't there.

It must have fallen down behind the bed when he had broken free. He crossed the wooden floor to the built in wardrobes that lined one wall of his blue bedroom and opened the sliding doors. He took down a fresh black shirt and put it on, tucking it into his trousers, and then chose a black leather belt and threaded it through the loops and fastened it.

He went barefoot from his apartment, locking the door behind him and pocketing the keys, and was silent as he passed Snow's room.

The last thing he needed was Snow questioning him. Javier didn't doubt that the old vampire would have heard Lilah and him. Snow didn't like the presence of humans in this area of the theatre.

It tended to awaken his bloodlust and make him frenzied with hunger to tear into them and drain them to death.

Javier knocked lightly on the mahogany panelled door of Antoine's room and listened closely. It was still dark out so Antoine should have been awake.

No sound came from the room on the other side of the door though.

He moved on, heading down the stairs to the offices. Antoine's door was open and his voice drifted out, a one sided conversation. He was on the phone.

Javier knocked on the open door, waited for the aristocrat vampire seated behind the huge oak desk in the darkly decorated office to acknowledge him with a wave of his hand, and then entered. He took the seat opposite Antoine and waited.

Antoine's pale blue eyes shifted to him and he ended his call, setting his mobile phone down on the table. The aristocrat vampire swept the lengths of his brown hair back, leaned into his black leather chair and loosed a long sigh.

"Did you see the show tonight?" Antoine said, his deep voice a mixture of accents that made his nationality hard to place.

Javier had never asked what family he and Snow belonged to. When they had started Vampirerotique, Antoine had told him and Callum that their family were all dead and that was that. Antoine and Snow were connected in society though, and it was their names on the theatre licence that drew the aristocrats to the shows.

Javier nodded. "I saw some of it."

"Victor seemed unusually relaxed during the final act." Antoine's icy blue eyes penetrated Javier's. "It wouldn't have had anything to do with what happened with Lord Ashville's ward, would it?"

"Lilah confirmed that she hit Victor, but only because Victor had been trying to tear Nia's throat open. The man lost control, Antoine. He deserved what he got."

Antoine sighed, tipped his head back and stared at the ceiling. "I suppose you are right... it is policy that our performers don't interact with the staff... it is odd though, Javier... I recall having a similar policy regarding the owners and staff."

Javier tensed when Antoine's gaze slowly drifted down to settle on him.

"She is an owned human, Javier. I had hoped that Snow was wrong and he did not smell her outside his room, and he did not smell you on her... but you reek of woman and sex."

Javier swallowed, fear crushing his chest. Antoine could easily kill him. At over one thousand years old and of pure blood, he was one of the most powerful vampires Javier knew, even more powerful than Lord Ashville.

"Lilah is the reason I am here to speak with you." Javier somehow managed to keep his fear from his voice. It was surprisingly steady. "Lord Ashville's claim on her is either false or incomplete."

"What do you mean?" Antoine sat forwards and leaned his elbows on his desk, creasing his silver-grey tailored shirt.

"She has her own will. She seduced me, could bear my touch and my bite with no ill effect." It was hard to lie to his old friend but he had to maintain the charade for Lilah's sake. She believed that it would save him and he was starting to hope that it would.

"Impossible."

"Not impossible at all. Ask her yourself. She will tell you that what we did has not pained her at all and that she was the one to initiate things between us. I just need you to send word to the heads of society about this and let them deal with it. Question us if you must. Please... if Lord Ashville comes... do not let him take Lilah and do not let him carry out punishment on me." Javier stood with the intent of convincing Antoine to go with him to Lilah and speak to her.

A sense of panic surged through the theatre bare seconds before Callum rushed into the office.

"We have a problem," Callum said, his green eyes wide and fear coming off him in waves.

Javier stared at him, his heart squeezed tight by icy claws, and sensed the pain in his blood before he heard her scream.

"Lilah!"

CHAPTER 8

Lilah woke alone in the middle of Javier's huge four-poster bed in his elegant blue room. She stretched, muscles tight and aching from making love with him, and smiled to herself.

The windowless room gave her no clue as to the hour.

Had the sun risen yet?

If it had, she was sure that Javier would be beside her, sound asleep. Sleeping curled in his arms had felt so good. She had never felt so safe.

Her life before Lord Ashville had bonded with her had been rough, living day to day with little comfort, scrounging for food and money on the street. After Lord Ashville had given her blood and taken her to his mansion, her life had scarcely improved. She had become a slave.

But then he had sent her here, to Javier, and she had fallen in love. During her past two years here, there had been times when he had been especially nice to her. Now she knew why.

Now she knew what love was.

Love was the way he had held her in his arms as she slept and watched over her, keeping her safe from the darkness in the world.

Protecting her.

Her heart hurt at the thought of him fighting Lord Ashville. She knew that he intended to fight for her. It was better than him letting her master enact the punishment for the law he had broken, but she still feared it.

Lilah pushed the thick feather duvet aside and rose from the bed. She rounded the foot of it, gathering her clothes as she went, and headed for the open door to the bathroom. The rich gold fixtures shone in the light when she flicked the switch, revealing the expansive room. The curved glass door of the double shower was open.

A shiver of arousal tripped through her at the thought of what Javier would have looked like had she taken longer to reach his room and caught him in the shower instead.

The image of him with wet sandy brown hair, water dripping from the haphazard spikes and rolling down his bare chest, was too delicious to contemplate without arousing herself.

She took one of the black towels off the white marble counter around the large oval sink and raised it to her nose. It smelt like Javier. Warm and spicy. She touched his shaving things and then his aftershave bottles that lined the back of the counter below the large rectangular mirror.

He had quite the collection of the same fragrance but she supposed it made sense.

It was annoying enough to a human when their favourite scent was no longer available and they had to find a new one. She couldn't imagine how many times a vampire had to find a new fragrance.

Especially one who was over six hundred years old.

Lilah couldn't even imagine what the world had been like when he had been born.

To a vampire father and a turned mother.

She hadn't missed the look in Javier's dark eyes when he had spoken of them and his sister's recent marriage to a man she had turned into a vampire. He wanted that for them. It frightened her but there was already a part of her that wanted to let him turn her so they could have their forever.

If they survived what was coming.

Lilah pressed her hand to her bare chest and focused on her heart and her blood, trying to sense her master. She clung to the hope that the wretched man was nowhere near and hadn't felt what she had done with Javier. It would give them time to track him down and speak to him. They couldn't hide from him forever. When she saw him again, she would make him release her so she could be with Javier.

She stepped into the shower and turned on the water. The pulsing beat of hot water over her skin chased some of her tension away and she closed her eyes and raised her face into it.

The sound of the door to the apartment opening made her pause and then smile. Javier. She had promised they would shower later so she remained under the jet, waiting for him to come to her. She heard his footsteps on the tiled floor of the white bathroom and turned with a wide smile to face the curved glass doors as they opened.

"Where did you go—"

Her eyes met dark red ones. She stared at them, every inch of her trembling despite the hot water cascading over her back.

Lord Ashville grabbed her wrist in a bruising grip and yanked her from the shower. She slipped on the floor and slammed onto it, banging her knee and elbow. It didn't stop her master. He dragged her along the floor until she managed to scramble onto her feet. She clawed at his hand on her wrist, trying to prise his fingers open, but it only made him tighten his grip until her bones creaked.

Lilah cried out.

"Shut up," Lord Ashville snapped, his fiery red eyes scalding her. He raised his arm, dragging hers upwards, and her feet left the floor, her shoulder threatening to pop out of its socket.

"Please... it hurts," Lilah whimpered and shivered, fear thundering in her chest, turning her stomach.

His eyes darkened, almost as black as his short hair, cruelty marring his youthful face.

"I told you to shut up." He snarled and threw her across the bedroom.

She hit the dressing table and collapsed into a heap, pain blazing through every inch of her, burning fiercest in her shoulder and hip.

He stalked towards her, blurring in and out of focus as she struggled to remain conscious, and crouched, grabbed her by her throat, and dragged her onto her feet.

Lilah choked and flailed her legs, kicking wildly. He grunted when she managed to catch him in the balls and dropped her. She made a break for the broken door but he reached it before her, blocking her way with his broad build. Lilah backed into the room, desperately searching for something to use as a weapon.

Unsurprisingly there was nothing she could use to dispatch a vampire. There were only things that would probably annoy him even more.

A letter opener on the bedside table, a wooden chair in the corner, an empty glass decanter on the dressing table.

All of them were within her reach if she moved quickly enough but none of them would stop him.

She tried for the letter opener but Lord Ashville came up behind her and caught her by her throat. The feel of his fingertips against her jugular stopped her dead. He pulled her hair aside so roughly that her head went with it, her neck cracking under the force, and snarled.

"Who did this?" His other hand scratched the marks on her throat and she whimpered again, afraid that he would cut her open with his nails. "Who violated you?"

"No one violated me," Lilah whispered and then grimaced when Lord Ashville sniffed the marks. "I chose to be with him. I initiated it!"

"Impossible." Lord Ashville grabbed her arm again and pulled her towards the corridor.

She made a desperate reach for the splintered doorframe and clung to it, grimacing as he yanked on her other arm. Her fingers slipped and she hit the deck with another violent bang.

It didn't stop Lord Ashville. He dragged her across the wooden floorboards in the corridor until she managed to get back onto her feet. Lilah redoubled her efforts and clawed at his hand, drawing blood with her nails. It didn't even slow him down.

He tugged her down the stairs and she stumbled, her heart pounding and tears filling her eyes.

The air of the theatre chilled her bare damp skin and she hung her head, hiding behind the wet lengths of her dark hair as they reached an area where humans and vampires were still at work.

Shame burned her cheeks as she felt everyone staring at her naked body and bile burned up her throat. She covered her privates with her free hand, giving up her fight against her master.

"Tell me where he is." Lord Ashville shook her and she cried out again when his claws pressed into her wrist, drawing blood.

"Never," Lilah spat the word at him and he threw her down the remaining few stairs ahead of him.

She hit the floor with a sharp bump and curled into a ball, holding herself. Tears streamed down her cheeks and over her nose.

"On your feet, bitch." He grabbed her upper arm, pulled her back up, and pushed her forwards, forcing her to keep moving.

The staff clearing the stage props scattered when Lord Ashville shoved the doors to the theatre open. He lifted Lilah and pushed her onto the stage before leaping onto it himself.

"Call out for him." He stalked towards her. She shuffled backwards on the dusty wooden stage, her hip aching as it pressed into it and pain splintering her skull.

Lilah shook her head. Lord Ashville slapped her and she screamed.

"There we go. That wasn't so difficult, was it?" He crouched next to her, his dark eyes full of cold cruelty as he looked down on her. "It will be over soon. The man who violated you will pay."

Lilah lay on the stage, panting and afraid, trembling and aching all over. She didn't want Javier to come. Lord Ashville would fight him.

She couldn't lose Javier.

"I started it," she muttered and swallowed, the taste of her own blood in her mouth making her feel sick. She weakly pushed herself up on her hands and then her knees. "I wanted him... and I seduced him."

"Liar." He caught her under the jaw and lifted her off the stage, holding her suspended by her neck. She choked as he squeezed, blocking her airway.

"Put the woman down." The male voice was a dark commanding snarl that echoed around the theatre.

Her eyes wildly sought the owner of it.

A man with white jaw length hair and eyes the colour of ice stood at the back of the stage, his broad figure swathed in a long black coat.

"I will not tolerate this behaviour. Set her down or I will kill you where you stand." Snow walked forwards, his face a dark mask that warned he wasn't joking. "I am sure there is a reasonable explanation for what has happened here. The woman says that she started things between herself and the vampire. I can vouch that she did."

"Are you the vampire?" Lord Ashville said and Snow shook his head. "Then stay out of it. It is none of your business."

"I assure you, as owner of this theatre and therefore a man responsible for the care of this woman, it is my business." Snow moved faster than Lilah could take in and she was suddenly in his arms, his long black coat around her shoulders, covering her nudity.

Lord Ashville stared at his empty hands and then glared at Snow.

He snarled and lunged at Snow.

Lilah threw herself into his path, unwilling to allow another innocent person to be dragged into this mess because of her, and screamed as Lord Ashville's backhand connected with the side of her head and sent her crashing into darkness.

CHAPTER 9

Javier entered the theatre in time to see Lilah collapse in the middle of the stage between Lord Ashville and Snow. The large white-haired male vampire roared at Lord Ashville but didn't get a chance to attack. Antoine was behind him in a heartbeat, restraining his arms, struggling to hold his brother back.

Every muscle on Snow's broad bare chest rippled with power and Antoine grunted as he fought to keep him restrained.

Callum raced in behind Javier and stopped dead when Lord Ashville's dark eyes fell on him. They shifted between Javier and Callum.

"Which of you is the vampire who violated my human?" Lord Ashville stepped towards Lilah's prone form. "If you do not tell me, I will force it out of you."

Before Javier could utter a word, Lord Ashville grabbed Lilah and shook her so hard that Javier feared he would kill her. Javier growled at the same time as Snow did. Lord Ashville looked at Javier and dropped Lilah back onto the hard wooden stage.

"You?" Lord Ashville pointed at him.

Javier nodded. "Lilah came to me. It was her decision. Our feelings are mutual. Your sway over her was not complete and it never was. Your bond with her was false and you do not own her, so you cannot come here to ask for my head. She initiated it and we broke no law."

He mounted the stage and stared at Lilah, using his senses to check her over. Her blood whispered her pain to him and her pulse was steady but too weak.

It frightened him and a deep desire to gather her into his arms and take her somewhere safe filled him.

She needed care.

She needed his blood.

It would help her heal the internal damage her bastard master had done to her because of him and would stop her wounds from bleeding. The scent of her blood in the air was only fuelling his rage and desire to make Lord Ashville pay.

"You are all liars. I know what I felt. You are forcing her to say these things to protect you." Lord Ashville went to grab her again and Javier snapped.

He threw himself at Lord Ashville, slamming into his side and sending them both crashing hard onto the wooden stage.

"Don't you touch her again!" Javier rolled on top of him and punched him hard, knocking his head to one side.

A second later he was sailing through the air and landing with a resounding thud next to Lilah.

He wheezed as he sucked air into his bruised lungs, looked across at her and reached his hand out, wanting to touch hers.

She was too far away.

Still beyond his grasp.

Lord Ashville's expensive leather shoe slamming into his gut caused him to double over and cough up blood. The taste of it in his mouth brought his fangs down and he snarled, grabbed Lord Ashville's leg and twisted it, sending the man spinning in the air.

He landed on the other side of Lilah, got to his feet and went to grab her again.

Snow roared, broke free of Antoine's arms and barrelled into Lord Ashville.

The scent of blood in the air grew stronger and a glistening dark patch spread across the front of Lord Ashville's black shirt as he distanced himself from the furious male vampire.

"God damn it, Snow!" Antoine threw himself at his brother but Snow sidestepped and launched himself at Lord Ashville again, baring his fangs at the same time.

Javier wasn't fast enough to intercept Snow and neither was Antoine. Snow swept his hand out as he passed a stunned Lord Ashville, his claws cutting across the side of the man's throat, and came around behind him, his hand poised to puncture his back.

Antoine slammed into Snow and the pair of them hit the stage, Snow snarling at his brother and trying to break free. Javier kicked Lord Ashville in the kneecap, grabbed his short dark hair and brought his head down onto his own knee, cracking it hard.

Lord Ashville stumbled backwards and Javier didn't give him a chance to recover, or let Snow intervene again. He appreciated the help of the powerful aristocrat vampire, wasn't about to question why Snow was attacking Lord Ashville, but he needed to be the one to deal with Lilah's master. The man would pay for hurting her tonight and for bonding with her against her will.

He would die by Javier's hand.

Antoine managed to subdue Snow enough that the snarling stopped. Javier didn't spare them a glance as he circled with Lord Ashville, his eyes on his enemy, waiting for the man to make his move. Blood drenched the front of his black shirt and coated the side of his neck.

Snow's attacks had given Javier a chance. They had weakened Lord Ashville enough that he might be able to defeat him now.

Javier came around close to Lilah. She still lay on the floor, unconscious and bleeding. He had to end this quickly and tend to her. The scent of her blood and the pain he had felt in her spoke to the more savage side of himself, forcing his eyes to switch to crimson and his fangs to extend further.

He sensed Callum move onto the stage and approach her, and a dark part of himself wanted to snarl and force the elite male to back away and leave her alone.

The rest of his heart overruled it, silently begging his close friend to pull Lilah to a safer distance before things turned bloody and more dangerous than they already were.

Lord Ashville's attention switched from Javier to Callum and he could see that he was going to attack in order to keep Lilah in the midst of their battle.

Javier wouldn't allow that to happen. He mustered all of his strength and attacked first, catching Lord Ashville off guard and forcing him backwards with each punch and swipe of his claws. Snow growled again and Javier glanced down to realise they had moved too close to him.

Lord Ashville made him pay for his momentary distraction, shredding his shirt with his claws and slicing down his chest.

Javier leapt backwards and snarled, pain blazing outwards from each long scratch. The feel of blood sliding down his stomach, sticking his shirt to his skin, unleashed his savage side.

He roared and threw himself at Lord Ashville, tackling him so they both landed close to Snow.

Snow swiped at them both, his blood-tinted eyes wild with hunger, and Antoine growled as he struggled to pin his older brother to the wooden stage floor.

Javier rolled with Lord Ashville, scratching and kicking, trying to gain the upper hand. His arms and chest blazed white-hot with each slice of Lord Ashville's claws over his flesh. Blood soaked the stage around them and filled the air, driving them both into a frenzy.

Callum reappeared from the side of the stage and joined Antoine in his struggle to calm Snow. The vampire was a danger to them all now. Javier rolled backwards, flipping Lord Ashville over his head, and landed on top of him. He punched Lilah's master, one strike after another, bloodying his face and satisfying the dark need to avenge her.

Lord Ashville grabbed him by the throat, fingers closing around it, throttling him. Javier didn't stop. Driven by the smell of blood and his lust for violence, he fought on regardless of the lack of air. He clawed and scratched at Lord Ashville's chest until his vision swam and the edges of his sight turned fuzzy and black.

Lord Ashville grinned up at him, rolled to his side and came out on top again. He throttled Javier and rather than fighting him, Javier fought for air instead. He grasped Lord Ashville's wrists, trying to prise his hands off his throat, and choked.

Someone moved out of the corner of his eye and then Lilah was standing over them both.

She brought a thick carved wooden pillar that normally held a church candle down on Lord Ashville's back, sending him slamming forwards into Javier's chest.

Lord Ashville reared up and turned on her.

He lashed his arm out, catching her across the stomach and sending her flying into the black painted wall to the side of the stage.

She fell to the floor in a heap.

Lord Ashville went after her.

Javier pushed himself onto his feet with great effort and shot as fast as he could across the stage after Lord Ashville, intent on reaching him before he could harm Lilah again.

He would never allow that.

Lilah was his now and he would do all in his power to protect her.

She was his.

He brought his fingers together so they formed a flat surface with his palm, extended his claws, and came up behind Lord Ashville. The man choked as Javier struck, driving his hand into his back and smashing through his ribs.

Javier growled, clutched Lord Ashville's heart, and tore it out.

Lord Ashville slumped to his knees and then fell forwards onto the stage floor.

Javier uncurled his fist and let the heart roll from his fingers and fall onto its former owner.

Blood dripped from his fingertips.

Javier stumbled past Lord Ashville's corpse, his body aching with each weary step, pain blazing across each long gash that littered his arms and chest. He fixed his senses on Lilah, needing to feel that she was alive and would heal with his blood in her body.

He collapsed onto his knees next to her and struggled to pull her into his arms.

They trembled and shook, weak from the fight and blood loss.

He still couldn't believe what he had done. There would be repercussions. He shouldn't have killed Lord Ashville. He should have retained enough control that he could have forced the man to face the heads of society and let them judge whether he and Lilah had broken the sacred law.

There was no hope of that now.

His superiors would believe he had sought to defend himself when he should have meekly accepted his fate and allowed Lord Ashville to collect his head. He had only made things worse.

He managed to work Lilah into his arms and rested there with her, his hands looped around her front and her back against his knees. Her soft steady breathing concerned him as much as her slow heartbeat. He closed his eyes and fought his own desire to sleep. He had to get her to safety and heal her.

"Let me help," Callum said and Javier snarled at him, baring his fangs, and held Lilah closer, unwilling to let anyone touch her while she was badly injured.

"She will live." Those words, roughly spoken by Snow, ignited the spark of hope in his chest and soothed some of his fear. He looked up at the powerful male, right into his icy eyes that were still ringed with red, needing to hear him say it again.

Antoine stood a step behind Snow, his pale blue eyes on his brother, wary and watchful, as though he expected him to lose control again at any moment. Snow glanced over his shoulder at his younger brother and Antoine's gaze shifted from him, to Callum and then down at Javier and finally Lilah.

"I will need to speak to our rulers about this," Antoine said and Javier nodded, unwilling to dare hope that they would grant him a reprieve.

They were likely to sentence him to death when they learned of what he had done and the cold look in Antoine's eyes said that he wouldn't do anything about it.

Javier hadn't expected anything less of Antoine.

The aristocrat believed in the laws and the sanctity of them, and they had never been close to each other. The man held himself at a distance from everyone except his brother. If it was Snow in his situation, Javier was sure that Antoine would lie to protect him.

Snow frowned at Lilah and spoke so quietly that Javier was sure he had misheard him. "I will deal with it."

Antoine stared at his brother.

Javier and Callum did too.

Snow lifted his head and looked down at Javier. "I will take responsibility for what happened here."

Javier wasn't sure what to say.

Snow crouched beside Lilah, a strange look in his now blue eyes. "You are like family to us."

Javier glanced at Antoine to find the man scowling at the back of his older brother's head.

He didn't seem to share Snow's view and Javier was certain that Snow wasn't taking responsibility because he felt Javier was like a brother to him.

He was dreadfully certain that Snow was seeking his death.

"It was my fault. I will take responsibility for my own actions. You are needed here more than I am and perhaps if I take Lilah with me to them they will see that we are telling the truth and that Lord Ashville had no true claim to her," Javier said and Snow shook his head. "I will not hear of it,

Snow. Let Antoine speak to them and then I will take Lilah to see them. All will be well."

"Let him, Brother." Antoine's tone was as black as midnight skies in winter and Javier could understand his anger. If Javier was in his position and it was his brother offering to face a board of vicious purebloods in place of another vampire, he would have been angry too. He would do all that he could to stop him. "I will contact them and then I will take Javier and Lilah to them personally. You need not involve yourself."

"I attacked him too." Snow straightened and his icy irises slid to one side, towards his brother, but he didn't turn to face him. He looked down at Lilah again and then turned away, heading for the stage exit. "You owe me, Javier. Tend to your pretty female and take care of her. She is yours now. Cherish the gift of her love."

The sound of the stage door slamming echoed around the theatre and Javier stared at it for long seconds before it opened again and Antoine stormed out of it, heading after his brother.

Javier looked down at Lilah where she lay in his arms and hoped with all of his heart that he was wrong about Snow, and that justice would be kind and protect him from the wrath of their rulers if he wasn't and Snow was seeking his death.

Antoine would never forgive him if their rulers executed Snow.

The aristocrat vampire would come for his head, or offer it in exchange for his brother's life.

He glanced up at Callum.

The look in his green eyes was one of reassurance and Javier accepted the kind gift. He looked towards the door, his mind on what Snow had done for him. He had known the aristocrat brothers for a century now, had witnessed their closeness and the lengths they would go to in order to protect each other.

A soothing wave rolled through him and he released the fear in his heart.

Antoine would never come for his head because he would never allow his brother to face their rulers alone. He would travel wherever Snow chose to go, even into the jaws of Hell, and would ensure his brother returned safely. He would lie to protect him, would back up Snow's story and blame this whole mess on bloodlust and an accidental killing, never mentioning the sacred law that had been broken.

Javier only hoped their rulers believed them. He wasn't sure how to thank Snow for what he was doing for him. He owed the vampire his life.

Cherish the gift of her love.

He would do just that.

Now that Lilah was his.

Javier slowly rose to his feet, lifting Lilah into his aching arms at the same time, ignoring the pain that tore through him.

He would suffer pain one hundred times stronger for her sake if he had to.

He would have faced their rulers and whatever sentence they would have given him now that he knew she was free of her master and safe.

Callum held the door for him and waited while he walked towards him, each step more painful than the last.

He would tend to his female.

He would cherish her forever if she would have him.

CHAPTER 10

Lilah woke slowly, her head strangely free of pain and her body warm and relaxed.

Why had she expected to wake in agony?

She fluttered her eyes open and Javier came into focus, lying next to her on his back, his face littered with thin red lines and bruises.

His lip was swollen and split, and there was a nasty dent in his nose.

She frowned and lowered her gaze to what she could see of his bare chest. More red lines marred his shoulders and torso. There had been a fight. Was that why she had expected to wake in pain?

She slowly raised her hands from under the midnight blue covers and frowned at them. They were dirty and there were cuts on them, but they were healing and had already passed the scab stage. Each mark was like a dark pink scar, several weeks' old rather than mere hours.

There were more marks on her dirty elbows and she could feel that her lip had split too, but it wasn't swollen like Javier's.

She touched it and then her cheek, recalling that Lord Ashville had dragged her through the theatre searching for Javier and everything had turned chaotic.

Lilah sat up abruptly and pain speared through her this time. She pressed her hands to her stomach and held down the bile and her urge to be sick.

Her vision swam and she waited for it to stop wavering before she looked around Javier's blue bedroom.

The long black coat folded neatly over the chair in the corner told her that part of her memories had been real. Snow had tried to protect her.

Had he killed Lord Ashville?

Her gaze tracked back to Javier where he slept beside her. Every cut and bruise on his beautiful face and body told her that he had been the one to fight for her. Had he killed her master? She placed her hand over her chest between her bare breasts and tried to feel Lord Ashville in her blood.

Her eyes widened.

She felt something but it didn't make her skin crawl and the presence was close to her. In this room.

Lilah touched her lips and then drew her hand away and stared at it and the healing cuts on her arms. The bruises on her skin were faded too, and she could no longer feel the internal pain from Lord Ashville's abusive behaviour towards her.

Javier had given his blood to her.

"Forgive me," Javier uttered in a raspy voice and slowly opened his chocolate brown eyes. Concern touched his expression and he wearily raised his hand and brushed his knuckles across her cheek. The worry in his eyes turned to fatigue and his hand drooped, falling to her breast, as though he no longer had the strength to lift it. She took hold of his hand for him and brought it to her face, holding it there so he could stroke it. "I wanted to give you a choice this time."

Lilah closed her eyes and pressed her cheek against his hand, feeling his apology deep in her blood. She wasn't angry with him. He had only given her blood so she would heal rapidly and he had probably saved her life by doing so.

When Lord Ashville had thrown her against the wall, she had felt her life forced from her body, the pain so intense that her heart had struggled. She had expected to never wake at all. Javier hadn't forced a bond upon her, not in the way Lord Ashville had.

He had gifted her with life by giving his blood to her and she could feel in her veins that he wished there had been another way to save her.

"There's nothing to forgive." She drew his hand away from her face. Her gaze fell to the deep bite mark on his wrist, a mark that he must have made for her. She pressed a long kiss to it, thankful for the gift that he had given her, a chance to be with him. Her heart whispered that he would never use the bond between them against her or treat her as Lord Ashville had done. He had given her blood out of love not out of a desire to own her. "I would have done the same for you."

She looked at the cuts and bruises on his body.

"I will do the same for you." She leaned over him on the bed, reached around behind her neck and pulled the hair away from her throat, revealing it to him.

Javier stared at her throat and then at the other side where he had bitten her. "You have no bite marks other than my own."

Lilah frowned and then shrugged. "You were the first to bite me."

"On your neck... or ever?" Javier struggled onto his elbows, propping himself up on the bed. The covers slid downwards to reveal the top of his stomach, the taut muscles enticing her to look at them. She kept her eyes on his, giving him the attention he deserved and refusing to gawp at him when he was having a serious conversation with her.

"Ever."

"Lord Ashville never took your blood?"

Lilah shook her head. "No. He was never interested in me like that. He only ever bit the men and slept with them."

Javier stared at her, slack jawed, his amazement running through her blood.

Lilah realised why he looked so surprised. "That's why he didn't have full control of me. You were apologising because you had taken my blood and then given me yours. That's what completes a bond between a human and their vampire master. That's why I still had my free will. He didn't have my blood to complete the bond."

Javier nodded. "I have never been so thankful in my life."

He didn't look as though he had much reason to be thankful right now. He was a mess and there were dark areas on the bedclothes where he had bled on them.

"What happened?" Lilah carefully traced along the edge of one of the cuts on his cheek and then furrowed her eyebrows when she ghosted her finger over his broken nose. The dark shadowing under his left eye extended down over his cheek to his jaw. "Did you kill him?"

"I didn't mean to," Javier whispered, his voice hoarse, and Lilah looked down at his throat and the dark purple bruises on it. It looked as though someone had strangled him. Her eyes briefly widened when she remembered coming around and seeing her master throttling Javier. It had driven her to move and she had grabbed the nearest heavy object and hit Lord Ashville with it to make him stop. "I snapped and killed him when he hit you again. It was only because of Snow that I managed it... and it is only because of Snow that I am here now."

Lilah frowned and looked at the black coat on the chair.

"Snow has decided to take my place and will face the consequences. He attacked Lord Ashville too and might have been the one to kill him if Antoine hadn't succeeded in restraining him."

The old vampire certainly was unpredictable. She had been surprised to see him there on the stage, telling her master to let her go or suffer death at his hands.

Javier seemed equally surprised that he had decided to take responsibility for what had happened.

"Will they kill him?" Lilah didn't want that and the look in Javier's eyes told her that he didn't either. She smiled and touched his cheek, hoping to chase away the pain in his body and his heart. "Maybe I need to take your mind off it."

Her echoing his earlier words to her brought a smile to his lips that became a grimace and he touched his split lip and the fresh blood that glistened on it.

Lilah slid her hand around the nape of his neck and helped him to sit up. She curled up beside him, so her bare breasts touched his chest and his arm, and guided him to her throat.

"Drink from me, Javier. Heal yourself," she whispered and he kissed her throat, sending shivers racing down her spine with each sweep of his lips over her skin.

Lilah closed her eyes and relaxed so it wouldn't hurt as much when he bit her.

He opened his mouth and licked the curve of her throat, and then gently sank his fangs into her. Her hands tensed against his back but she didn't flinch. She refused to when she had offered this to him. The initial stab of pain faded with his first slow pull on her blood and his second sent liquid heat surging into her veins.

She settled her cheek against his and held him close to her, caressing his strong back and listening to him feeding from her vein. It didn't disgust her as she had always thought it would.

There was something sensual about it, something beautiful as the connection between them opened again, stronger than ever this time.

He withdrew his fangs and continued to drink, his hands coming to press into her spine, clutching her to him as his strength returned.

She looked down at his back and watched in fascination as the wounds on it healed before her eyes, the fresh blood in his veins accelerating the process more than she had thought it would.

Each mouthful of blood he drew from her caused it to quicken, until only dark pink lines marked his skin, scars like she had on hers.

Javier licked her throat, murmuring something in Spanish against it, and she couldn't hide her surprise when he drew back and she saw that the cuts and bruises on his face had healed.

Only faint scars remained and a darker streak over his nose where it had been broken. She touched his throat, glad to see the horrific bruises there were gone.

"Thank you," he whispered and kissed her before she could tell him that she should be the one thanking him for freeing her from Lord Ashville. She kissed him instead, silently thanking him with each sweep and caress of her lips against his. She could feel he was still worried about what had happened between them and wasn't surprised when he broke the kiss and cupped her cheek, staring deep into her eyes. "I won't act on the bond between us. If you want to leave the theatre, you can do so. You are free, Lilah. You can do as you please."

"I can do as I please?" She rose to her knees.

A pained look crossed his face when she slipped down from the bed on the bathroom side and it turned to confusion when she held her hand out to him.

"You are not leaving?"

Lilah couldn't stop herself from laughing aloud at that. "Never... but I am going to do as I please... and it pleases me that you join me in the shower, as promised."

Javier smiled and it warmed her to see it and the affection and happiness in his dark brown eyes. He was by her side in an instant, his hand in hers, leading her towards his en-suite bathroom.

Lilah stared unabashedly at his bare bottom as he walked, loving the way it dimpled with each step, so firm and tempting. He jolted when she ran her hand over it and gave it a pat.

"Why do I have the feeling you will be playing the role of master in this relationship?" He grinned over his shoulder at her, pulled her into his arms so her front pressed against his, and lifted her.

She didn't protest as he carried her into the large shower cubicle, his hands firmly gripping her backside. She was actually looking forward to him being in command but she had enjoyed tying him up.

Perhaps they could alternate between dominant and submissive, because just the thought of chaining him up properly with shackles he couldn't easily break had her hot as Hell.

Javier pressed her into the cool tiles of the shower, deftly flicked the water on, and kissed her. He wasn't the only one getting feelings. Lilah had the feeling that she wasn't going to get to scrub the dirt off her body before Javier had had his wicked way with her.

He didn't seem to notice any of his healing cuts as he lifted her legs and wrapped them around his waist. His hardening cock nudged her bottom as he kissed her, dominating her mouth and plundering it with his tongue.

He tasted like blood but she couldn't bring herself to care. Her tongue tangled with his, licking its cool length as her fingers tangled in his hair, holding his mouth against hers.

She moaned when he shifted his hips backwards, allowing his erection to rise between them, and then ground against her.

"Are you sure you're up for this?" she whispered into his mouth and he thrust against her again, telling her without words that he was definitely up for something.

Lilah moaned and closed her eyes as he kissed down her jaw to her throat and found the marks he had placed on her just minutes before. He closed his mouth over them and sucked, reopening the puncture wounds, drawing more blood from her.

The combination of his cock rubbing her aroused nub and his mouth working on her throat had her burning up and tipping her head back into the hard white tiles of the shower.

The hot water beat down on her side, cascading over her skin.

Javier thrust again, his fingers pressing into her backside, pinning her against the wall. He groaned and she bucked her hips into his, rubbing herself on his hard cock, loving the feel of it pressing against her. He licked her neck in response and devoured it with hungry kisses.

"I want you," he whispered and nibbled her earlobe, lightly biting it. "My Lilah."

Lilah smiled at that and the passion and intense need behind those two words. She held him to her, stroking his hair, melting into him as he kissed her throat and held her hard against his body as though he would never let her go now that he had her. She didn't want him to.

"I want you too," she said and he groaned when she kissed his shoulder. When she bit down on it with her blunt teeth, his groan became a feral growl and his grip on her tightened so much that she let out a squeak. She had forgotten that it was dangerous to bite him when she had him worked up. "My Javier."

He growled again, the possessive edge to it thrilling her, and shifted his hips against hers, nudging the head of his cock into her folds and brushing her clit with it.

She moaned and raised herself up him and then slid downwards again, catching the crown of his length and forcing it down with her. It pressed close to her slick channel, teasing her with how near he was to entering her.

It felt like miles away to her as she tried to shift him closer, ached to be one with him again.

Javier's hand left her hip, guided his cock down to her entrance, and then he eased her onto it, slowly impaling her. The delicious sting of his hard length entering her, stretching her body to perfection, was blissful.

She closed her eyes and captured Javier's lips, kissing him as he withdrew and then thrust back into her, each stroke long and slow, filling her with more than desire.

The connection between them through their blood was open, their minds as one as their bodies joined them, until she wasn't sure where he ended and she began. She could feel all his love for her and how much he needed her.

Each slow meeting of their hips, each careful stroke of his cock and word murmured against her lips between kisses, spoke to her of his fear during the fight with Lord Ashville, his devotion to her, and his intense need.

Those feelings echoed within her heart and soul, perfectly matching his. She had been so afraid for him, had feared that she would lose him and that this bliss they had found would come to a terrible end.

She loved him so much, needed him more than air and would do anything to be with him.

Anything.

"Javier, look at me," she whispered and he moved back, slowly pumping her, his hands gentle against her hips.

His eyes met hers and warmth flooded her, deep affection making her feel as though she was drowning in this moment, floating away on a sea of ecstasy. She moaned as he moved deeper inside her, his pelvis brushing her sensitive nub, and struggled to keep her eyes open.

She looked into his, feeling open to him, laid bare by the connection between their blood and their bodies. "Yes."

He frowned. "Yes?"

Lilah smiled and stroked his cheek, her gaze falling to his mouth as she swept her thumb across his lower lip before rising to meet his again. Her heart trembled in her throat, a timid thing that she hoped wouldn't make him think that she didn't mean what she was about to say because she meant it with her heart and her soul.

"Yes. It's my answer."

Javier groaned and thrust harder into her, as though that would clear her head and make her explain things. She moaned instead, losing her mind a little and forgetting what she was supposed to be saying.

She writhed against him, her hands clutching his shoulders, and fought to keep sane enough.

Perhaps she should have waited until after they had collapsed sated on his bed before bringing it up.

"Lilah," he whispered on a moan and breathed deep, his thrusts slowing again, the longer strokes doing nothing to clear her head. "What are you saying?"

"You asked me..." Heaven could she even get the words out without gasping each one on a moan? Her stomach tightened, body involuntarily clenching his cock as her arousal soared, her hunger driving her. She wanted to climax again, needed it so fiercely. Needed Javier so fiercely. "Would I consent..."

It was no use. She couldn't get it out when Javier was making love to her, the pleasure of it driving her out of her head.

Javier went deathly still, his wide eyes telling her that he had figured out the question she had been answering.

"You want to become a vampire?" When he said it so bluntly, in a voice that echoed his shock, it brought a blush to her cheeks and made her think twice about it.

"Yes." That word was easy to say when she knew the joy it would bring them both. "I want you to turn me because I love you, Javier, and I want that forever you spoke about."

Javier groaned and then kissed her breathless, his body still within hers.

She smiled against his mouth, feeling his love flowing into her but unwilling to let him get away without saying the words to her too.

She raised herself and he moaned again when he met her down thrust, plunging his cock into her, restarting what they had been doing before she had interrupted his stroke. He kept things slow and tender, each kiss against her lips conveying his love for her. It still wasn't enough.

"Will you?" she whispered against his mouth and he drew back again, staring deep into her eyes.

"I will," he said with a wide smile and she moaned when he thrust into her again, struggling to keep her mind on track when she wanted to tell him to go faster and harder, to shatter the tight ball of energy gathering in her abdomen and give her a taste of bliss in his arms again. "I love you, Lilah... and I will have my forever with you."

He brushed his mouth over hers, their tongues tangling as he drove into her, harder now, building her towards a climax that she knew would be the moment her life changed forever. Each long stroke of his cock, each brush of his pelvis against her clit, sent a tiny ripple of pleasure chasing along her thighs.

She clung to him, kissing him, losing herself in the warmth of his feelings as they filled her mind, joining with hers.

It was beautiful.

She gasped into his mouth as her body tightened around his, clenching his cock as he plunged it deep into her, and a thousand tiny sparks exploded outwards from her core, heating her through and sending her trembling.

Javier held her to him, his length throbbing within her, his mouth dropping to her throat.

Lilah closed her eyes and held Javier, tangling her fingers in his hair, melting in his strong embrace. She wasn't afraid of him. He wasn't a monster.

He was the man that she loved and she wanted to be with him forever, wanted that fairytale ending that he had spoken to her about with the same ferocity as he did.

He had fought for her and she had fought for him, and they had made it through together.

It was truly beautiful.

Javier wrapped his lips around her throat.

They had promised each other forever.

Lilah tipped her head back and sighed as his fangs entered her.

And he sealed it with an eternal kiss.

The End

Read on for a preview of the next book in the London Vampires romance series, Crave!

CRAVE

Three weeks had passed since Callum had left London and headed to Paris to scout for performers for a new show at the theatre he ran with three other vampires, and it had been one week since he had last emailed Antoine, the aristocrat pureblood in charge of overseeing the performances at Vampirerotique.

He should have contacted him again by now. It wasn't as though Callum hadn't thought about it. He had booted up his laptop and started to type out the email every morning before retiring for the day. Yesterday, he had even reached the point of typing in his name at the end of the email before deleting the entire thing.

Callum leaned his back against the brass rail that edged the curved dark mahogany bar top, his green gaze scanning the occupants of the crowded room, picking out viable prey, potential performers, and identifying the species of each person his eyes fell on.

Part of him was still working and it was that part that kept whispering that Antoine wouldn't be angry with him for disappearing.

If he just dropped a brief email or even a text message stating that he was still looking for performers but hadn't spotted anyone worthy of joining the Vampirerotique family in the past week then Antoine would probably forgive him for disobeying his command to contact him daily.

It would be a lie though.

He had seen several vampires, both male and female, at the nightclubs he had been moving between for the past three weeks.

All of them would work well in the theatre and draw the crowds.

They were exhibitionists who had been more than comfortable performing private acts in front of the gathered dancers. There had been males who had groped and grinded with their human female prey, and female vampires who had engaged in acts just a whisper away from screwing in the open booths where anyone could see them.

All of them had been worthy of him approaching them and giving them the hard sell.

Not many of their type refused to audition when they gained an all expenses paid trip to London and the chance to try out for a place in a famous theatre.

There was one female who had stood out amongst the usual crowd last week. She was perfect for the new show that Antoine had in mind, could easily be the star performer, but Callum couldn't bring himself to approach her and whenever he thought about mentioning her to Antoine, a knot formed deep in his gut.

Callum had ignored the feeling and just satisfied himself with watching her in the club. He had first seen her with another female, one that he had approached during a lull towards the end of the evening. She had eagerly accepted his offer of an audition, even though she knew the sort of place his theatre was and that it didn't normally look for performers from her species.

Werewolf.

When Antoine had first told him that he would be departing for Paris in search of new talent, and that it wouldn't just be the usual scouting mission this time but would include seeking werewolves for a special performance, Callum had almost choked on his glass of blood.

Vampirerotique had never hired werewolves before. In fact, he was certain that in the hundred years they had been running the theatre, there had never been a werewolf on stage. Their kind rarely interacted with each other, unless you counted the occasional war. Werewolves didn't like vampires. The feeling was more than mutual.

Callum had sent three werewolves to audition so far, all female as requested.

This female would be perfect for the show too. She would steal it and make it hers, just as she stole the attention of the entire club as she moved through it with sensual grace that had the eyes of every male and some females on her, and made Callum think about some therianthropes he had met in the past. She had the moves of a feline shifter rather than a werewolf.

Callum could easily imagine her moving on the stage, how she would sidle over to the large vampire males and bring them to their knees with only a seductive sway of her hips and flash of a sultry smile.

Hell, she had Callum on his knees. He had been following her for a week now, shunning his duty in favour of tracking her down each night and watching her from a distance.

His new private pleasure.

The club she had chosen tonight catered to a mixed crowd, although the humans didn't know that.

One of the male bartenders was a shifter, one was human, and one was a vampire.

That surprised Callum.

He had never thought he would live to see a vampire working alongside a shifter, but the two young males seemed to get along. He couldn't sense any bad feelings between them so it wasn't an act put on for the sake of the patrons and the human bartender.

Callum's gaze tracked the female through the club, studying how she slid between the dancers, occasionally stopping to work her body against a male.

She smiled wickedly at a young human man as he caught her wrist and pulled her against him, twisting her so her back pressed against his front.

She wriggled her hips and raised her hands above her head as she slid down the length of her partner and then back up again, almost as tall as he was in her heeled black boots. Her tight dark jeans emphasised lean long legs that Callum had rather disturbingly dreamed about since first seeing her, imagining their slender strong lengths wrapped around his backside as he fucked her.

He had dreamed about pushing the loose flowing material of her empire-line top up to reveal the toned plane of her stomach and then kissing it, feeling her body shift beneath him, before continuing and peeling the high waist tucked under her breasts over their full firm globes. He had dipped his head and captured each sweet dusky bud in turn, swirling his tongue around and sucking them until she moaned low in appreciation.

The brunette female werewolf moved on, thanking her temporary partner with a brief brush of her rosy lips across his cheek and a saucy stroke of her palm over his crotch that had Callum ready to speed onto the dance floor and rip the human to shreds.

She was his.

He drew a long slow breath to calm himself, focusing on it and not her, waiting for the need to pass. If he looked at her now, he would be on the dance floor before he realised what he was doing and would be tugging her into his arms, using all of his strength to make it clear to her that she belonged to him now.

Callum shook his head to rid it of the desire to dance with her and feel her body pressing into his, hot and supple under his questing hands. He wouldn't let her go as easily as the male human had.

He watched her move through the dancers again, twirling and smiling, her wavy soft brown hair dancing with her, tumbling over her shoulders and breasts. Each time she lifted her bare arms in the air, the hem of her top rose, revealing a tantalising flash of her stomach or back. Her jeans rode low on her hips, barely covering her backside and crotch.

She was a vixen, a real predator as she glanced over every man, even those with partners, looking for tonight's fun. He had seen her leave with a new man every night.

A strange urge to follow her and see what she did with them had built inside him until he had no longer been able to resist the need to know.

It wasn't what he had thought it would be and an even stranger feeling had swept through him on realising that she was luring males away to feed on them.

Like his kind, werewolves enjoyed the taste of blood and needed it to survive, although they could supplement their need with nourishment from food.

Unlike his kind, werewolves couldn't turn a human. Her bite wouldn't change the human into a werewolf. Once she had finished with the man, she had wiped his memory and left him in the alley.

Callum had almost followed her home but had forced himself to return to his hotel instead. The sight of her feeding had given him some seriously erotic dreams and he had woken tonight with a raging erection that hadn't gone down until he had tended to it.

It was coming back as he watched her, his thoughts diving down routes they shouldn't be taking. A vampire had no place desiring a werewolf.

Desiring?

Hell, this hunger went beyond desire and ran deeper in his veins than lust.

He craved her.

Callum turned and flagged down the vampire bartender. The blond man smiled knowingly, nodded, and took down a martini glass. He filled it to the brim with dark liquid that was black in the flashing purple and blue lights of the club and stuck a cherry on a stick in it.

Callum held out a twenty euro note at the same time as the vampire placed the glass down on an elegant white napkin and slid it across the bar to him.

"I'll take one of those," a female voice said right beside him, "and tall, dark and sexy here is paying."

He was?

Callum frowned and turned to say that he damn well wasn't paying for her drink and froze as his eyes fell on the female werewolf. He felt the vampire bartender's gaze on him, sensed him waiting to see what Callum's reply would be. Callum glanced at him and nodded.

The vampire made up another glass of blood, stuck a cherry in it, and slid it over to her before moving away.

The werewolf raised her glass in a salute to Callum, sipped the blood, and set it back down on the napkin. Her bloodstained lips curved into a wicked sultry smile.

Callum was smitten.

She leaned closer, her bare left elbow resting on the bar, and ran her fingertips down his dark purple silk tie. Her smile widened when she curled her fingers around it, drew it away from his black tailored shirt, and tugged him towards her.

"You've been watching me like I'm a bitch in heat and you're an alpha. What gives?" She wasn't French as he had expected.

Her accent was as British as his own.

Callum calmly removed her hand from his tie, straightened it out and smoothed it down. "I'm just here on business, and I'm definitely not an alpha. I'm a vampire."

She smiled and tilted her head to one side, causing the long waves of her brown hair to shift across her breasts and cover the tempting display of cleavage the tight section of her black sleeveless top created.

"A vampire with a definite hard-on for a species most of his kind would see as disgusting and forbidden," she said over the rapid beat of the music, lifted the cocktail stick and cherry from her drink, and popped it into her mouth.

Callum's gaze narrowed on her mouth, transfixed by the sight of her sucking the cherry.

She parted her lips and withdrew the glossy red fruit, dipped it back into her blood and swirled it around before raising it back to her mouth and teasing him by licking the crimson liquid off it again.

His chest tightened and he struggled to breathe as the tip of her tongue flicked over the cherry, swirling around it.

She slowly slid the fruit into her mouth, lips puckering as she sucked, her eyes closing in what looked like pleasure to him.

The sight of her ratcheted his hunger up another notch, flooding him with a deep throbbing ache to feel her tongue brushing his in the way it had the cherry, to have her mouth on his flesh and to run his lips over every inch of her bare skin and drive her wild until she was sobbing his name and begging for more.

"I don't have a hard-on for your species... just you." Callum moved faster than she could evade, catching the wrist of the hand she held the cocktail stick in, pulling it away from her lips and claiming them for his own.

She responded instantly, her tongue thrusting past his lips and teeth to slide along his. He slanted his head, slipped his other arm around her slim waist and dragged the full length of her body against his as he seized control of the kiss.

She melted against him, as supple and hot as he had dreamed she would be, her breasts pressing into his hard chest, the heat of her driving him to the edge.

He tangled his tongue with hers, swallowing her breathy gasps as he dominated her, crushing each attempt she made to reclaim control. Her fight only made him burn hotter for her, made him use his strength on her and tighten his grip on her wrist and side.

Her gasps became low rumbling moans.

The firmer he was with her, the more of his strength he used, the lower they became and the more she struggled, as though she wanted to feel how much more powerful he was than her.

She liked it.

The female werewolf snapped out of his grasp and slapped him so hard across his cheek that he couldn't fail to realise where he had gone wrong.

His fangs cut into his lower lip.

He hadn't noticed them extending.

Before he could explain to her that it was just the heat of the moment that had brought them out and that he hadn't intended to bite her, she was striding away from him, heading back towards the busy dance floor.

Callum growled, swiftly drank his martini glass of blood to take the edge off his hunger and followed her, intent on explaining and tasting her again.

The crowd kept closing behind her, blocking his way and frustrating him.

He pushed through them, his senses tracking her so he didn't lose her again.

She wasn't heading out of the club at least. The expansive dark club only had one exit and that was the other way, beyond the bar. She was either heading towards the booths that lined the edges of the room or the dance floor itself.

Was she planning on losing him in the throng of people?

It would be difficult to track her in amongst so many signatures. There were several other werewolves in the club tonight. Their presence would help mask hers even though he knew her scent now, had instinctively put it to memory when kissing her. Devil, she had tasted so wicked and delicious.

Callum licked the faint trace of blood off his lips and finally broke through the crowd around the bar, coming out near the edge of the dance floor. The heavy beat of the music pounded through his body, thrumming in his veins, pushing the tension mounting inside him, the need to find her and have her in his arms again.

The need to taste her lips.

He scoured the dancers and spotted her heading closer to the DJ. The lights flashed brightest there, hurting his eyes, and the volume of the music would be unbearable that close to the speakers.

She knew vampires well.

Her species could move around during the day so they weren't as sensitive to light and her hearing wasn't as acute when she was in her human form. She stopped there and danced with a male.

He couldn't tell whether her partner was human or werewolf, but he was immense, taller and broader than Callum was.

She had intentionally chosen a place that would hurt him and had now selected a partner who could easily protect her. Her wiliness told Callum that the male would be a werewolf.

He only wondered why she no longer looked confident. Her gaze constantly darted about as she danced with the man, her body held at a distance from his, as though she was afraid to get any closer. Why would she fear her own kind?

That question and the challenge she had issued by choosing to dance with an immense werewolf in an area that was uncomfortable for Callum drove him onto the dance floor.

He moved through the crowd, his gaze constantly on her, studying her face and the flicker of fear that was gradually surfacing in her eyes. The usual confident shine in them was gone by the time he was within a few metres of her.

The male werewolf caught her shoulders, turned her around and dragged her back against his bulky body, caging her there with a thick forearm across her stomach.

His black t-shirt stretched over an obscene amount of muscle and Callum considered the insanity of approaching such a male. Although he was likely older than the werewolf, and vampires were inherently more powerful, his build was almost slender compared to him and he was a good few inches shorter too.

That could be an advantage though.

A lower centre of gravity gave him a more solid footing than his monolithic rival and his slimmer build gave him the advantage of speed. He could probably incapacitate the werewolf with only minimal injury to himself.

However.

There were two other male werewolves seated on the curved dark leather seat of the booth behind the male dancing with the woman, and both of them were watching the couple. Three glasses stood on the oval black table in the centre of the booth. The male was with them.

One werewolf he might be able to handle.

Three would crush him.

It should have stopped him from pursuing the woman, but his feet still propelled him forwards, towards what could only be a bloody and painful future.

He couldn't turn back now that he had tasted her.

He hungered for another touch, another taste.

He craved her.

And he would have her.

CRAVE

His mind has been set on his work for the past one hundred years. Now a forbidden beauty has stolen his attention and is threatening to steal his heart too.

Callum has come to the city of romance on business, not pleasure, but when he sets eyes on a gorgeous werewolf in a nightclub, he can't ignore the dark carnal craving she ignites in him. His work for Vampirerotique, the erotic theatre he runs with three other vampires, can wait. The only thing that matters now is satisfying his sinful hunger for a woman who most vampires would consider an enemy.

Kristina is on the run from her pack. Her alpha is intent on forcing her to bear his child and she's not about to live through the same nightmare as her mother had. When a tall, dark and sexy vampire catches her eye, she can't believe the ferocity of the desire he unleashes in her or the fact that she enjoys the feel of his eyes on her and his silent pursuit of her in the clubs each night.

When Kristina finally gets a taste of Callum in a forbidden kiss, will she be strong enough to resist the allure of the vampire and his offer to share his bed for a week of unbridled, wild sex, or will she surrender to her own craving for the safety and passion she finds in his embrace?

Available now in ebook and paperback

ABOUT THE AUTHOR

Felicity Heaton is a New York Times and USA Today best-selling author who writes passionate paranormal romance books. In her books she creates detailed worlds, twisting plots, mind-blowing action, intense emotion and heart-stopping romances with leading men that vary from dark deadly vampires to sexy shape-shifters and wicked werewolves, to sinful angels and hot demons!

If you're a fan of paranormal romance authors Lara Adrian, J R Ward, Sherrilyn Kenyon, Gena Showalter, Larissa Ione and Christine Feehan then you will enjoy her books too.

If you love your angels a little dark and wicked, her best-selling Her Angel romance series is for you. If you like strong, powerful, and dark vampires then try the Vampires Realm romance series or any of her stand alone vampire romance books. If you're looking for vampire romances that are sinful, passionate and erotic then try her London Vampires romance series. Or if you like hot-blooded alpha heroes who will let nothing stand in the way of them claiming their destined woman then try her Eternal Mates series. It's packed with sexy heroes in a world populated by elves, vampires, fae, demons, shifters, and more. If sexy Greek gods with incredible powers battling to save our world and their home in the Underworld are more your thing, then be sure to step into the world of Guardians of Hades.

If you have enjoyed this story, please take a moment to contact the author at **author@felicityheaton.com** or to post a review of the book online

Connect with Felicity:
Website – http://www.felicityheaton.com
Blog – http://www.felicityheaton.com/blog/
Twitter – http://twitter.com/felicityheaton
Facebook – http://www.facebook.com/felicityheaton
Goodreads – http://www.goodreads.com/felicityheaton
Mailing List – http://www.felicityheaton.com/newsletter.php

FIND OUT MORE ABOUT HER BOOKS AT:
http://www.felicityheaton.com

Printed in Great Britain
by Amazon